Mystery House

Mickey Spillane

EVERYBODY'S WATCHING ME

Mystery House
California

EVERYBODY'S WATCHING ME

For more titles in the Mystry House library,
visit our website: **www.FictionHousePress.com**

"Everybody's Watching Me" was published in *Manhunt* as a 4-part serial in the January, February, March, and April 1953 issues. Copyright 1952-53 by Eagle Publications Inc. No renewal.

First Mystery House edition August 2021

ISBN 978-1-64720-388-7

Fiction House Press
www.FictionHousePress.com

Part One

The killers were afraid of Vetter, and their fear made them anxious to hunt him down and kill him. But how do you hunt a man nobody's ever seen?

I HANDED the guy the note and shivered a little bit because the guy was as big as they come, and even though he had a belly you couldn't get your arms around, you wouldn't want to be the one who figured you could sink your fist in it. The belly was as hard as the rest of him, but not quite as hard as his face.

Then I knew how hard the back of his hand was because he smashed it across my jaw and I could taste the blood where my teeth bit into my cheek.

Maybe the guy holding my arm knew I couldn't talk because he said, "A guy give him a fin to bring it, boss. He said that."

"Who, kid?"

I spit the blood out easy so it dribbled down my chin instead of going on the floor. "Gee, Mr. Renzo . . ."

His hand made a dull, soggy crack on my skin. The buzz got louder in my ears and there was a jagged, pounding pain in my skull.

"Maybe you didn't hear me the first time, kid. I said who."

The hand let go my arm and I slumped to the floor. I didn't want to, but I had to. There were no legs under me any more. My eyes were open, conscious of only the movement of ponderous things that got closer. Things that moved quickly and seemed to dent my side without causing any feeling at all.

That other voice said, "He's out, boss. He ain't saying a thing."

"I'll make him talk."

"Won't help none. So a guy gives him a fin to bring the note. He's not going into a song and dance with it. To the kid a fin's a lot of dough. He watches the fin and not the guy."

"You're getting too damn bright," Renzo said.

"That's what you pay me for being, boss."

"Then act bright. You think a guy hands a note like this to some kid? Any kid at all? You think a kid's gonna bull in here to deliver it when he can chuck it down a drain and take off with the fin?"

"So the kid's got morals."

"So the kid knows the guy or the guy knows him. He ain't letting no kid get away with his fin." The feet moved away from me, propped themselves against the dark blur of the desk. "You read this thing?" Renzo asked.

"No."

"Listen then. 'Cooley is dead. Now my fine fat louse, I'm going to spill your guts all over your own floor.' " Renzo's voice droned to a stop. He sucked hard on the cigar and said, "It's signed, *Vetter*."

You could hear the unspoken words in the silence. That hush that comes when the name was mentioned and the other's half-whispered "Son of a bitch they were buddies, boss?"

"Who cares? If that crumb shows his face around here, I'll break his lousy back. Vetter, Vetter, Vetter. Everyplace you go that crumb's name you hear."

"Boss, look. You don't want to tangle with that guy. He's killed plenty of guys. He's. . . ."

"He's different from me? You think he's a hard guy?"

"You ask around, boss. They'll tell you. That guy don't give a damn for nobody. He'll kill you for looking at him."

"Maybe in his own back yard he will. Not

here, Johnny, not here. This is my city and my back yard. Here things go my way and Vetter'll get what Cooley got." He sucked on the cigar again and I began to smell the smoke. "Guys what pull a fastie on me get killed. Now Cooley don't work my tables for no more smart plays. Pretty soon the cops can take Vetter off their list because he won't be around no more either."

"You going to take him, boss?" Johnny said.

"What do you think?"

"Anything you say, boss. I'll pass the word around. Somebody'll know what he looks like and'll finger him." He paused, then, "What about the kid?"

"He's our finger, Johnny."

"Him?"

"You ain't so bright as I thought. You should get your ears to the ground more. You should hear things about Vetter. He pays off for favors. The errand was worth a fin, but he's gonna look in to make sure the letter got here. Then he spots the kid for his busted up face. First time he makes contact we got him. You know what, Johnnie? To Vetter I'm going to do things slow. When they find him the cops get all excited but they don't do nothing. They're glad to see Vetter dead. But other places the word gets around, see? Anybody can bump Vetter gets to be pretty big and nobody pulls any more smart ones. You understand, Johnny?"

"Sure, boss. I get it. You're going to do it yourself?"

"Just me, kid, just me. Like Helen says I got a passion to do something myself and I just got to do it. Vetter's for me. He better be plenty big, plenty fast and ready to start shooting the second we meet up."

It was like when Pop used to say he'd do something and we knew he'd do it sure. You look at him with your face showing the awe a kid gets when he knows fear and respect at the same time and that's how Johnny must have been looking at Renzo. I knew it because it was in his voice too when he said, "You'll do it, boss. You'll own this town lock, stock and gun butt yet."

"I own it now, Johnny. Never forget it. Now wake that kid up."

This time I had feeling and it hurt. The hand that slapped the full vision back to my eyes started the blood running in my mouth again and I could feel my lungs choking on a sob.

"What was he like, kid?" The hand came down again and this time Renzo took a step forward. His fingers grabbed my coat and jerked me off the floor.

"You got asked a question. What was he like?"

"He was . . . big," I said. The damn slob

choked me again and I wanted to break something over his head.

"How big?"

"Like you. Bigger'n six. Heavy."

Renzo's mouth twisted into a sneer and he grinned at me. "More. What was his face like?"

"I don't know. It was dark. I couldn't see him good."

He threw me. Right across the room he threw me and my back smashed the wall and twisted and I could feel the tears rolling down my face from the pain.

"You don't lie to Renzo, kid. If you was older and bigger I'd break you up into little pieces until you talked. It ain't worth a fin. Now you start telling me what I want to hear and maybe I'll slip you something."

"I . . . I don't know. Honest, I . . . if I saw him again it'd be different." The pain caught me again and I had to gag back my voice.

"You'd know him again?"

"Yes."

Johnny said, "What's your name, kid?"

"Joe . . . Boyle."

"Where do you live?" It was Renzo this time.

"Gidney Street," I told him. "Number three."

"You work?"

"Gordon's. I . . . push."

"What'd he say?" Renzo's voice had a nasty

tone to it.

"Gordon's a junkie," Johnny said for me. "Has a place on River Street. The kid pushes a cart for him collecting metal scraps."

"Check on it," Renzo said, "then stick with him. You know what to do."

"He won't get away, boss. He'll be around whenever we want him. You think Vetter will do what you say?"

"Don't things always happen like I say? Now get him out of here. Go over him again so he'll know we mean what we say. That was a lousy fin he worked for."

After things hurt so much they begin to stop hurting completely. I could feel the way I went through the air, knew my foot hit the railing and could taste the cinders that ground in my mouth. I lay there like I was pressed out, waiting for the pain to come swelling back, making sounds I didn't want to make. My stomach wanted to break loose but couldn't find the strength and I just lay there cursing guys like Renzo who could do anything they wanted and get away with it.

Then the darkness came, went away briefly and came back again. When it lost itself in the dawn of agony there were hands brushing the dirt from my face and the smell of flowers from the softness that was a woman who held me and said, "You poor kid, you poor kid."

My eyes opened and looked at her. It was like something you dream about because she was the kind of woman you always stare at, knowing you can't have. She was beautiful, with yellow hair that tumbled down her neck like a torch that lit up her whole body. Her name was Helen Troy and I wanted to say, "Hello, Helen," but couldn't get the words out of my mouth.

Know her? Sure, everybody knew her. She was Renzo's feature attraction at his Hideaway Club and her picture was all over town. But I never thought I'd get to have my head in her lap.

There were feet coming up the path that turned into one of the men from the stop at the gate and Helen said, "Give me a hand, Finney. Something happened to the kid."

The guy she called Finney stood there with his hands on his hips shaking his head. "Something'll happen to you if you don't leave him be. The boss gives orders."

She tightened up all over, her fingers biting into my shoulder. It hurt but I didn't care a bit. "Renzo? The pig!" She spat it out with a hiss. She turned her head slowly and looked at me. "Did he do this, kid?"

I nodded. It was all I could do.

"Finney," she said, "go get my car. I'm taking the kid to a doctor."

"Helen, I'm telling you . . ."

"Suppose I told the cops . . . no, not the cops, the feds in this town that you have holes in your arms?"

I thought Finney was going to smack her. He reached down with his hand back but he stopped. When a dame looks at you that way you don't do anything except what she tells you to.

"I'll get the car," he said.

She got me on my feet and I had to lean on her to stay there. She was just as big as I was. Stronger at the moment. Faces as bad off as mine weren't new to her, so she smiled and I tried to smile back and we started off down the path.

We said it was a fight and the doctor did what he had to do. He laid on the tape and told me to rest a week then come back. I saw my face in his mirror, shuddered and turned away. No matter what I did I hurt all over and when I thought of Renzo all I could think of was that I hoped somebody would kill him. I hoped they'd kill him while I watched and I hoped it would take a long, long time for him to die.

Helen got me out to the car, closed the door

after me and slid in behind the wheel. I told her where I lived and she drove up to the house. The garbage cans had been spilled all over the sidewalk and it stank.

She looked at me curiously. "Here?"

"That's right," I told her. "Thanks for everything."

Then she saw the sign on the door. It read, ROOMS. "Your family live here too?"

"I don't have a family. It's a rooming house."

For a second I saw her teeth, white and even, as she pulled her mouth tight. "I can't leave you here. Somebody has to look after you."

"Lady, if . . ."

"Ease off, kid. What did you say your name was?"

"Joe."

"Okay, Joe. Let me do things my way. I'm not much good for anything but every once in awhile I come in handy for something decent."

"Gee, lady . . ."

"Helen."

"Well, you're the nicest person I've ever known."

I said she was beautiful. She had the beauty of the flashiest tramp you could find. That kind of beauty. She was like the dames in the big shows who are always tall and sleepy looking and who you'd always look at but wouldn't marry or take home to your folks. That's the kind of beauty she had. But for a long couple of seconds she seemed to grow a new kind of beauty that was entirely different and she smiled at me.

"Joe . . ." and her voice was warm and husky, "that's the nicest thing said in the nicest way I've heard in a very long time."

My mouth still hurt too much to smile back so I did it with my eyes. Then something happened to her face. It got all strange and curious, a little bit puzzled and she leaned forward and I could smell the flowers again as that impossible something happened when she barely touched her mouth to mine before drawing back with that searching movement of her eyes.

"You're a funny kid, Joe."

She shoved the car into gear and let it roll away from the curb. I tried to sit upright, my hand on the door latch. "Look, I got to get out."

"I can't leave you here."

"Then where . . ."

"You're going back to my place. Damn it, Renzo did this to you and I feel partly responsible."

"That's all right. You only work for him."

"It doesn't matter. You can't stay there."

"You're going to get in trouble, Helen."

She turned and flashed me a smile. "I'm always in trouble."

"Not with him."

"I can handle that guy."

She must have felt the shudder that went through me.

"You'd be surprised how I can handle that fat slob," she said. Then added in an undertone I wasn't supposed to hear, "Sometimes."

It was a place that belonged to her like flowers belong in a rock garden. It was the top floor of an apartment hotel where the wheels all stayed in the best part of town with a private lawn twelve stories up where you could look out over the city and watch the lights wink back at you.

She made me take all my clothes off and while I soaked in a warm bath full of suds she scrounged up a decent suit that was a size too big, but still the cleanest thing I had worn in a long while. I put it on and came out in the living room feeling good and sat down in the big chair while she brought in tea.

Helen of Troy, I thought. So this is what she looked like. Somebody it would take a million bucks and a million years to get close to . . . and here I was with nothing in no time at all.

"Feel better, Joe?"

"A little."

"Want to talk? You don't have to if you don't want to."

"There's not much to say. He worked me over."

"How old are you, Joe?"

I didn't want to go too high. "Twenty-one," I said.

There it was again, that same curious expression. I was glad of the bandages across my face so she couldn't be sure if I was lying or not.

I said, "How old are you?" and grinned at her.

"Almost thirty, Joe. That's pretty old, isn't it?"

"Not so old."

She sipped at the tea in her hand. "How did you happen to cross Renzo?"

It hurt to think about it. "Tonight," I said, "it had just gotten dark. A guy asked me if I'd run a message to somebody for five bucks and I said I would. It was for Mr. Renzo and he told me to take it to the Hideaway Club.

"At first the guy at the gate wouldn't let me in, then he called down that other one, Johnny. He took me in, all right."

"Yes?"

"Renzo started giving it to me."

"Remember what the message said?"

Remember? I'd never forget it. I'd hope from now until I died that the guy who wrote it did everything he said he'd do.

"Somebody called Vetter said he'd kill Renzo," I told her.

Her smile was distant, hard. "He'll have to be a pretty tough guy," she said. What she said next was almost under her breath and she was staring into the night when she said it. "A guy like that I could go for."

"What?"

"Nothing, Joe." The hardness left her smile until she was a soft thing. "What else happened?"

Inside my chest my heart beat so fast it felt like it was going to smash my ribs loose. "I . . . heard them say . . . I would have to finger the man for them."

"You?"

I nodded, my hand feeling the soreness across my jaw.

She stood up slowly, the way a cat would. She was all mad and tense but you couldn't tell unless you saw her eyes. They were the same eyes that made the Finney guy jump. "Vetter," she said. "I've heard the name before."

"The note said something about a guy named Cooley who's dead."

I was watching her back and I saw the shock of the name make the muscles across her shoulders dance in the light. The tightness went down her body until she stood there stiff-legged, the flowing curves of her chest the only things that moved at all.

"Vetter," she said. "He was Cooley's friend."

"You knew Cooley?"

Her shoulders relaxed and she picked a cigarette out of a box and lit it. She turned around, smiling, the beauty I had seen in the car there again.

"Yes," Helen said softly, "I knew Cooley."

"Gee."

She wasn't talking to me any more. She was speaking to somebody who wasn't there and each word stabbed her deeper until her eyes were wet. "I knew Cooley very well. He was . . . nice. He was a big man, broad in the shoulders with hands that could squeeze a woman . . ." She paused and took a slow pull on the cigarette. "His voice could make you laugh or cry. Sometimes both. He was an engineer with a quick mind. He figured how he could make money from Renzo's tables and did it. He even laughed at Renzo and told him crooked wheels could be taken by anybody who knew how."

The tears started in the corners of her eyes but didn't fall. They stayed there, held back by pride maybe.

"We met one night. I had never met anyone like him before. It was wonderful, but we were never meant for each other. It was one of those things. Cooley was engaged to a girl in town, a very prominent girl."

The smoke of the cigarette in her hand swirled up and blurred her face.

"But I loved him," she said. With a sudden flick of her fingers she snapped the butt on the rug and ground it out with her shoe. "I hope he kills him! I hope he kills him!"

Her eyes drew a line up the floor until they were on mine. They were clear again, steady, curious for another moment, then steady again. I said, "You don't . . . like Renzo very much?"

"How well do you know people, Joe?"

I didn't say anything.

"You know them too, don't you? You don't live in the nice section of town. You know the dirt and how people are underneath. In a way you're lucky. You know it now, not when you're too old. Look at me, Joe. You've seen women like me before? I'm not much good. I look like a million but I'm not worth a cent. A lot of names fit me and they belong. I didn't get that way because I wanted to. He did it. Renzo. I was doing fine until I met him.

"Sure, some young kids might think I'm on top, but they never get to peek behind the curtain. They never see what I'm forced into and the kind of people I have to know because others don't want to know me. If they do they don't want anybody to know about it."

"Don't say those things, Helen."

"Kid, in ten years I've met two decent people. Cooley was the first." She grinned and the hate left her face. "You're the other one. You don't give a hang what I'm like, do you?"

"I never met anybody like you before."

"Tell me more." Her grin got bigger.

"Well, you're beautiful. I mean real beautiful. And nice. You sure are built . . ."

"Good enough," she said and let the laugh come out. It was a deep, happy laugh and sounded just right for her. "Finish your tea."

I had almost forgotten about it. I drained it down, the heat of it biting into the cuts along my cheek. "Helen . . . I ought to go home. If Mr. Renzo finds out about this, he's going to burn up."

"He won't touch me, Joe."

I let out a grunt.

"You either. There's a bed in there. Crawl into it. You've had enough talk for the night."

I woke up before she did. My back hurt too much to sleep and the blood pounded in my head too hard to keep it on the pillow. The clock beside the bed said it was seven-twenty and I kicked off the covers and dragged my clothes on.

The telephone was in the living room and I took it off the cradle quietly. When I dialed the number I waited, said hello as softly as I could and asked for Nick.

He came on in a minute with a coarse, "Yeah?"

"This is Joe, Nick."

"Hey, where are you, boy? I been scrounging all over the dump for you. Gordon'll kick your tail if you don't get down here. Two other guys didn't show . . ."

"Shut up and listen. I'm in a spot."

"You ain't kidding. Gordon said. . . ."

"Not that, jerk. You see anybody around the house this morning?"

I could almost hear him think. Finally he said, "Car parked across the street. Think there was a guy in it." Then, "Yeah, yeah, wait up. Somebody was giving the old lady some lip this morning. Guess I was still half asleep. Heard your name mentioned."

"Brother!"

"What's up, pal?"

"I can't tell you now. You tell Gordon I'm sick or something, okay?"

"Nuts. I'll tell him you're in the clink. He's tired of that sick business. You ain't been there long enough to get sick yet."

"Tell him what you please. Just tell him. I'll call you tonight." I slipped the phone back and turned around. I hadn't been as quiet as I thought I'd been. Helen was standing there in the doorway of her bedroom, a lovely golden girl, a bright morning flower wrapped in a black stem like a bud ready to pop.

"What is it, Joe?"

There wasn't any use hiding things from her. "Somebody's watching the house. They were looking for me this morning."

"Scared, Joe?"

"Darn right I'm scared! I don't want to get laid out in some swamp with my neck broken. That guy Renzo is nuts. He'll do anything when he gets mad."

"I know," Helen said quietly. Her hand made an unconscious movement across her mouth. "Come on, let's get some breakfast."

We found out who Vetter was that morning. At least Helen found out. She didn't cut corners or make sly inquiries. She did an impossible thing and drove me into town, parked the car and took a cab to a big brownstone building that didn't look a bit different from any other building like it in the country. Across the door it said, PRECINCT NO. 4 and the cop at the desk said the captain would be more than pleased to see us.

The captain was more than pleased, all right. It started his day off right when she came in and he almost offered me a cigar. The nameplate said his name was Gerot and if I had to pick a cop out to talk to, I'd pick him. He was in his late thirties with a build like a wrestler and I'd hate to be in the guy's shoes who tried to bribe him.

It took him a minute to settle down. A gorgeous blonde in a dark green gabardine suit blossoming with curves didn't walk in every day. And when he did settle down, it was to look at me and say, "What can I do for you?" but looking like he already knew what happened.

Helen surprised him. "I'd like to know something about a man," she said. "His name is Vetter."

The scowl started in the middle of his forehead and spread to his hairline.

"Why?"

She surprised him again. "Because he promised to kill Mark Renzo."

You could watch his face change, see it grow intense, sharpen, notice the beginning of a caustic smile twitch at his lips. "Lady, do you know what you're talking about?"

"I think so."

"You think?"

"Look at me," she said. Captain Gerot's eyes met hers, narrowed and stayed that way. "What do you see, Captain?"

"Somebody who's been around. You know the answers, don't you?"

"All of them, Captain. The questions, too."

I was forgotten. I was something that didn't matter and I was happy about it.

Helen said, "What do you think about Renzo, Captain?"

"He stinks. He operates outside city limits where the police have no jurisdiction and he has the county police sewed up. I think he has some of my men sewed up too. I can't be sure but I wish I were. He's got a record in two states, he's clean here. I'd like to pin a few jobs on that guy. There's no evidence, yet he pulled them. I know this . . . if I start investigating I'm going to have some wheels on my neck."

Helen nodded. "I could add more. It really doesn't matter. You know what happened to Jack Cooley?"

Gerot's face looked mean. "I know I've had the papers and the state attorney climb me for it."

"I don't mean that."

The captain dropped his face in his hands resignedly, wiped his eyes and looked up again. "His car was found with bullet holes in it. The quantity of blood in the car indicated that nobody could have spilled that much and kept on living. We never found the body."

"You know why he died?"

"Who knows? I can guess from what I heard. He crossed Renzo, some said. I even picked up some info that said he was in the narcotics racket. He had plenty of cash and no place to show where it came from."

"Even so, Captain, if it was murder, and Renzo's behind it, you'd like it to be paid for."

The light blue of Gerot's eyes softened dangerously. "One way or another . . . if you must know."

"It could happen. Who is Vetter?"

He leaned back in his chair and folded his hands behind his neck. "I could show you reams of copy written about that guy. I could show you transcripts of statements we've taken down and copies that the police in other cities have sent out. I could show you all that but I can't pull out a picture and I can't drop in a print number on the guy. The people who got to know him and who finally saw him, all seem to be dead."

My voice didn't sound right. "Dead?"

Gerot's hands came down and flattened on the desk. "The guy's a killer. He's wanted every place I could think of. Word has it that he's the one who bumped Tony Briggs in Chicago. When Birdie Cullen was going to sing to the grand jury, somebody was paid fifty thousand to cool him off and Vetter collected from the syndicate. Vetter was paid another ten to knock off the guy who paid him the first time so somebody could move into his spot."

"So far he's only a name, Captain?"

"Not quite. We have a few details on him but we can't give them out. That much you understand, of course."

"Of course. But I'm still interested."

"He's tough. He seems to know things and do things nobody else would touch. He's a professional gunman in the worst sense of the word and he'll sell that gun as long as the price is right."

Helen crossed her legs with a motion that brought her whole body into play. "Supposing, Captain, that this Vetter was a friend of Jack Cooley? Supposing he got mad at the thought of his friend being killed and wanted to do something about it?"

Gerot said, "Go on."

"What would you do, Captain?" The smile went up one side of his face. "Most likely nothing." He sat back again. "Nothing at all . . . until it happened."

"Two birds with one stone, Captain? Let

Vetter get Renzo . . . and you get Vetter?"

"The papers would like that," he mused.

"No doubt." Helen seemed to uncoil from the chair. I stood up too and that's when I found out just how shrewd the captain was. He didn't bother to look at Helen at all. His blue eyes were all on me and being very, very sleepy.

"Where do you come in, kid?" he asked me.

Helen said it for me. "Vetter gave him a warning note to hand to Renzo."

Gerot smiled silently and you could see that he had the whole picture in his mind. He had our faces, he knew who she was and all about her, he was thinking of me and wanted to know all about me. He would. He was that kind of cop. You could tell.

We stood on the steps of the building and the cops coming in gave her the kind of look every man on the street gave her. Appreciative. It made me feel good just to be with her. I said, "He's a smart cop."

"They're all smart. Some are just smarter than others." A look of impatience crossed her face. "He said something . . ."

"Reams of copy?" I suggested.

I was easy for her to smile at. She didn't have to look up or down. Just a turn of her head. "Bright boy."

She took my hand and this time I led the

way. I took her to the street I knew. It was off the main drag and the people on it had a look in their eyes you don't see uptown. It was a place where the dames walked at night and followed you into bars if they thought you had an extra buck to pass out.

They're little joints, most of them. They don't have neon lights and padded stools, but when a guy talks he says something and doesn't play games. There's excitement there and always that feeling that something is going to happen.

One of those places was called *The Clipper* and the boys from the *News* made it their hangout. Cagey boys with the big think under their hats. Fast boys with a buck and always ready to pay off on something hot. Guys who took you like you were and didn't ask too many questions.

My kind of people.

Bucky Edwards was at his usual stool getting a little bit potted because it was his day off. I got the big stare and the exaggerated wink when he saw the blonde which meant I'd finally made good about dragging one in with me. I didn't feel like bragging, though. I brought Helen over, went to introduce her, but Bucky said, "Hi, Helen. Never thought I'd see you out in the daylight," before I could pass on her name.

"Okay, so you caught a show at the Hideaway," I said. "We have something to ask you."

"Come on, Joe. Let the lady ask me alone."

"Lay off. We want to know about Vetter."

The long eyebrows settled down low. He looked at me, then Helen, then back at me again. "You're making big sounds, boy."

I didn't want anyone else in on it. I leaned forward and said, "He's in town, Bucky. He's after Renzo."

He let out a long whistle. "Who else knows about it?"

"Gerot. Renzo. Us."

"There's going to be trouble, sure."

Helen said, "Only for Renzo."

Bucky's head made a slow negative. "You don't know. The rackets boys'll flip their lids at this. If Vetter moves in here there's going to be some mighty big trouble."

My face started working under the bandages. "Renzo's top dog, isn't he?"

Bucky's tongue made a swipe at his lips. "One of 'em. There's a few more. They're not going to like Renzo pulling in trouble like Vetter." For the first time Bucky seemed to really look at us hard. "Vetter is poison. He'll cut into everything and they'll pay off. Sure as shooting, if he sticks around they'll be piling the cabbage in his lap."

"Then everybody'll be after Vetter," I said.

Bucky's face furrowed in a frown. "Uh-uh. I wasn't thinking that." He polished off his drink and set the empty on the bar. "If Vetter's here after Renzo they'll do better nailing Renzo's hide to the wall. Maybe they can stop it before it starts."

It was trouble, all right. The kind I wasn't feeling too bad about.

Bucky stared into his empty glass and said, "They'll bury Renzo or he'll come out of it bigger than ever."

The bartender came down and filled his glass again. I shook my head when he wanted to know what we'd have. "Good story," Bucky said, "if it happens." Then he threw the drink down and Bucky was all finished. His eyes got frosty and he sat there grinning at himself in the mirror with his mind saying things to itself. I knew him too well to say anything else so I nudged Helen and we walked out.

Some days go fast and this was one of them. She was nice to be with and nice to talk to. I wasn't important enough to hide anything from so for one day she opened her life up and fed me pieces of it. She seemed to grow younger as the day wore on and when we reached her apartment the sun was gilding her hair with golden reddish streaks and I was gone, all gone. For one day I was king and there wasn't any trouble. The laughter poured out of us and people stopped to look and laugh back. It was a day to remember when all the days are done with and you're on your last.

I was tired, dead tired. I didn't try to refuse when she told me to come up and I didn't want to. She let me open the door for her and I followed her inside. She had almost started for the kitchen to cook up the bacon and eggs we had talked about when she stopped by the arch leading to the living room.

The voice from the chair said, "Come on in, sugar pie. You too, kid."

And there was Johnny, a nasty smile on his mouth, leering at us.

"How did you get in here?"

He laughed at her. "I do tricks with locks, remember?" His head moved with a short jerk. "Get in here!" There was a flat, nasal tone in his voice.

I moved in beside Helen. My hands kept opening and closing at my side and my breath was coming a little fast in my throat.

"You like kids now, Helen?"

"Shut up, you louse," she said.

His lips peeled back showing his teeth. "The mother type. Old fashioned type, you know."

He leered again like it was funny. My chest started to hurt from the breathing. "Too big for a bottle, so . . ."

I grabbed the lamp and let it fly and if the cord hadn't caught in the wall it would have taken his head off. I was all set to go into him but all he had to do to stop me was bring his hand up. The rod was one of those Banker's Specials that were deadly as hell at close range and Johnny looked too much like he wanted to use it for me to move.

He said, "The boss don't like your little arrangement, Helen. It didn't take him long to catch on. Come over here, kid."

I took a half step.

"Closer."

"Now listen carefully, kid. You go home, see. Go home and do what you feel like doing, but stay home and away from this place. You do that and you'll pick up a few bucks from Mr. Renzo. Now after you had it so nice here, you might not want to go home, so just in case you don't, I'm going to show you what's going to happen to you."

I heard Helen's breath suck in with a harsh gasp and my own sounded the same way. You could see what Johnny was setting himself to do and he was letting me know all about it and there wasn't a thing I could do. The gun was pointing right at my belly even while he jammed his elbows into the arms of the chair to get the leverage for the kick that was going to maim me the rest of my life. His shoe was hard and pointed, a deadly weight that swung like a gentle pendulum.

I saw it coming and thought there might be a chance even yet but I didn't have to take it. From the side of the room Helen said, "Don't move, Johnny. I've got a gun in my hand."

And she had.

The ugly grimace on Johnny's face turned into a snarl when he knew how stupid he'd been in taking his eyes off her to enjoy what he was doing to me.

"Make him drop it, Helen."

"You heard the kid, Johnny."

Johnny dropped the gun. It lay there on the floor and I hooked it with my toe. I picked it up, punched the shells out of the chambers and tossed them under the sofa. The gun followed them.

"Come here, Helen," I said.

I felt her come up behind me and reached around for the .25 automatic in her hand. For a second Johnny's face turned pale and when it did I grinned at him.

Then I threw the .25 under the sofa too.

They look funny when you do things like

that. Their little brains don't get it right away and it stuns them or something. I let him get right in the middle of that surprised look before I slammed my fist into his face and felt his teeth rip loose under my knuckles.

Helen went down on her knees for the gun and I yelled for her to let it alone, then Johnny was on me. At least he thought he was on me. I had his arm over my shoulder, laid him into a hip roll and tumbled him easy. I didn't want too much noise.

I walked up. I took my time. He started to get up and I chopped down on his neck and watched his head bob. I got him twice more in the same place and Johnny simply fell back. His eyes were seeing, his brain thinking and feeling but he couldn't move. While he lay there, I chopped twice again and Johnny's face became blotched and swollen while his eyes screamed in agony.

I put him in a cab downstairs. I told the driver he was drunk and fell and gave him a ten spot from Johnny's own wallet with instructions to take him out to the Hideaway and deliver same to Mr. Renzo. The driver was very sympathetic and took him away.

Then I went back for Helen. She was sitting on the couch waiting for me, the strangeness back in her eyes. She said, "When he finished with you, he would have started on me."

"I know."

"Joe, you did pretty good for a kid."

"I was brought up tough."

"I've seen Johnny take some pretty big guys. He's awfully strong."

"You know what I do for a living, Helen? I push a junk car, loaded with iron. There's competition and pretty soon you learn things. Those iron loaders are strong gees too. If they can tumble you, they lift your pay."

"You had a gun, Joe," she reminded me.

And her eyes mellowed into a strange softness that sent chills right through me. They were eyes that called me closer and I couldn't say no to them. I stood there looking at her, wondering what she saw under the bandages.

"Renzo's going after us for that," I said.

"That's right, Joe."

"We'll have to get out of here. You, anyway."

"Later we'll think about it."

"Now, damn it."

Her face seemed to laugh at me. A curious laugh. A strange laugh. A bewildered laugh. There was a sparkling dance to her eyes she kept half veiled and her mouth parted just a little bit. Her tongue touched the tip of her teeth, withdrew and she said, "Now is for something else, Joe. Now is for a woman going back a long time who sees somebody she could have loved then."

I looked at her and held my breath. She was so completely beautiful I ached and I didn't want to make a fool of myself. Not yet.

"Now is for you to kiss me, Joe," she said.

I tasted her.

Part Two

Joe Boyle—with all eyes still on him, and with murder still dogging his footsteps. The reason? Vetter!

I WAITED until midnight before I left. I looked in her room and saw her bathed in moonlight, her features softly relaxed into the faintest trace of a smile, a soft, golden halo around her head.

They should take your picture like you are now, Helen, I thought. It wouldn't need a retoucher and there would never be a man who saw it who would forget it. You're beautiful, baby. You're lovely as a woman could ever be and you don't know it. You've had it so rough you can't think of anything else and thinking of it puts the lines in your face and that chiseled granite in your eyes. But you've been around and so have I. There have been dozens of dames I've thought things about but not things like I'm thinking now. You don't care what or who a guy is; you just give him part of yourself as a favor and ask for nothing back.

Sorry, Helen, you have to take something back. Or at least keep what you have. For you I'll let Renzo push me around. For you I'll let him make me finger a guy. Maybe at the end I'll have a chance to make a break. Maybe not. At least it's for you and you'll know that much. If I stay around, Renzo'll squeeze you and do it so hard you'll never be the same. I'll leave, beautiful. I'm not much. You're not much either. It was a wonderful day.

I lay the note by the lamp on the night table where she couldn't miss it. I leaned over and blew a kiss into her hair, then turned and got out of there.

Nobody had to tell me to be careful. I made sure nobody saw me leave the building and doublechecked on it when I got to the corner. The trip over the back fences wasn't easy, but it was quiet and dark and if anybody so much as breathed near me I would have heard it. Then when I stood in the shadows of the store at the intersection I was glad I had made the trip the hard way. Buried between the parked cars along the curb was a police cruiser. There were no markings. Just a trunk aerial and the red glow of a cigarette behind the wheel.

Captain Gerot wasn't taking any chances. It made me feel a little better. Upstairs there Helen could go on sleeping and always be sure of waking up. I waited a few minutes longer then drifted back into the shadows toward the rooming house.

That's where they were waiting for me. I knew it a long time before I got there because I had seen them wait for other guys before. Things like that you don't miss when you live around the factories and near the waterfronts. Things like that you watch and remember so that when it happens to you, it's no surprise and you figure things out beforehand.

They saw me and as long as I kept on going in the right direction they didn't say anything. I knew they were where I couldn't see them and even if I made a break for it, it wouldn't do me any good at all.

You get a funny feeling after a while. Like a rabbit walking between rows of guns wondering which one is going to go off. Hoping that if it does you don't get to see it or feel it. Your stomach seems to get all loose inside you and your heart makes too much noise against your ribs. You try not to, but you sweat and the little muscles in your hands and thighs start to jump and twitch and all the while there's no sound at all, just a deep, startling silence with a voice that's there just the same. A statue, laughing with its mouth open. No sound, but you can hear the voice. You keep walking, and the breathing keeps time with your footsteps, sometimes trying to get ahead of them. You find yourself chewing on your lips because you already know the horrible impact of a fist against your flesh and the uncontrollable spasms that come after a pointed shoe bites into the muscle and bone of your side.

So much so that when you're almost there and a hand grabs your arm you don't do anything except look at the face above it and wait until it says, "Where you been, kid?"

I felt the hand tighten with a gentle pressure, pulling me in close. "Lay off me. I'm minding my own. . ."

"I said something, sonny."

"So I was out. What's it to you?"

His expression said he didn't give a hang at all. "Somebody wants to know. Feel like taking a little ride?"

"You asking?"

"I'm telling." The hand tightened again. "The car's over there, bud. Let's go get in it, huh?"

For a second I wondered if I could take him or not and knew I couldn't. He was too big and too relaxed. He'd known trouble all his life, from little guys to big guys and he didn't fool easily. You can tell after you've seen a lot of them. They knew that some day they'd wind up holding their hands over a bullet hole or screaming through the bars of a cell, but until then they were trouble and too big to buck.

I got in the car and sat next to the guy in the back seat. I kept my mouth shut and my eyes open and when we started to head the wrong way, I looked at the guy next to me. "Where we going?"

He grinned on one side of his face and looked out the window again.

"Come on, come on, quit messing around! Where we going?"

"Shut up."

"Nuts, brother. If I'm getting knocked off I'm doing a lot of yelling first, starting right now. Where . . ."

"Shut up. You ain't getting knocked off." He rolled the window down, flipped the dead cigar butt out and cranked it back up again. He said it too easily not to mean it and the jumps in my hands quieted down a little.

No, they weren't going to bump me. Not with all the trouble they went to in finding me. You don't put a couple dozen men on a mug like me if all you wanted was a simple kill. One hopped up punk would do that for a week's supply of snow.

We went back through town, turned west

into the suburbs and kept right on going to where the suburbs turned into estates and when we came to the right one the car turned into a surfaced driveway that wound past a dozen flashy heaps parked bumper to bumper and stopped in front of the fieldstone mansion.

The guy beside me got out first. He jerked his head at me and stayed at my back when I got out too. The driver grinned, but it was the kind of face a dog makes when he sees you with a chunk of meat in your fist.

A flunky met us at the door. He didn't look comfortable in his monkey suit and his face had scar tissue it took a lot of leather-covered punches to produce. He waved us in, shut the door and led the way down the hall to a room cloudy with smoke, rumbling with the voices of a dozen men.

When we came in the rumble stopped and I could feel the eyes crawl over me. The guy who drove the car looked across the room at the one in the tux, said, "Here he is, boss," and gave me a gentle push into the middle of the room.

"Hi, kid." He finished pouring out of the decanter, stopped it and picked up his glass. He wasn't an inch bigger than me, but he had the walk of a cat and the eyes of something dead. He got up close to me, faked a smile and held out the glass. "In case the boys had you worried."

"I'm not worried."

He shrugged and sipped the top off the drink himself. "Sit down, kid. You're among friends here." He looked over my shoulder. "Haul a chair up, Rocco."

All over the room the others settled down and shifted into position. A chair seat hit the back of my legs and I sat. When I looked around everybody was sitting, which was the way the little guy wanted it. He didn't like to have to look up to anybody.

He made it real casual. He introduced the boys when they didn't have to be introduced because they were always in the papers and the kind of guys people point out when they go by in their cars. You heard their names mentioned even in the junk business and among the punks in the streets. These were the big boys. Top dogs. Fat fingers. Big rings. The little guy was biggest of all. He was Phil Carboy and he ran the West Side the way he wanted it run.

When everything quieted down just right, Carboy leaned on the back of a chair and said, "In case you're wondering why you're here, kid, I'm going to tell you."

"I got my own ideas," I said.

"Fine. That's just fine. Let's check your ideas with mine, okay? Now we hear a lot of things around here. Things like that note you delivered to Renzo and who gave it to you and what Renzo did to you." He finished his drink and smiled. "Like what you did to Johnny, too. That's all straight now, isn't it?"

"So far."

"Swell. Tell you what I want now. I want to give you a job. How'd you like to make a cool hundred a week, kid?"

"Peanuts."

Somebody grunted. Carboy smiled again, a little thinner. "The kid's in the know," he said. "That's what I like. Okay, kid. We'll make it five hundred per for a month. If it don't run a month you get it anyway. That's better than having Renzo slap you around, right?"

"Anything's better than that." My voice started getting chalky.

Carboy held out his hand and said, "Rocco . . ." Another hand slid a sheaf of bills into his. He counted it out, reached two thousand and tossed it into my lap. "Yours, kid."

"For what?"

His lips were a narrow gash between his cheekbones. "For a guy named Vetter. The guy who gave you a note. Describe him."

"Tall," I said. "Big shoulders. I didn't see his face. Deep voice that sounded tough. He had on a trench coat and a hat."

"That's not enough."

"A funny way of standing," I told him. "I saw Sling Herman when I was a kid before the cops got him. He stood like that. Always ready to go for something in his pocket the cops said."

"You saw more than that, kid."

The room was too quiet now. They were all hanging on, waiting for the word. They were sitting there without smoking, beady little eyes waiting for the finger to swing until it stopped and I was the one who could stop it.

My throat squeezed out the words. I went back into the night to remember a guy and drag up the little things that would bring him into the light. I said, "I'd know him again. He was a guy to be scared of. When he talks you get a cold feeling and you know what he's like." My tongue ran over my lips and I lifted my eyes up to Carboy. "I wouldn't want to mess with a guy like that. Nobody's ever going to be tougher."

"You'll know him again. You're sure?"

"I'm sure." I looked around the room at the faces. Any one of them a guy who could say a word and have me dead the next day. "He's tougher than any of you."

Carboy grinned and let his tiny white teeth show through. "Nobody's that tough, kid."

"He'll kill me," I said. "Maybe you too. I don't like this."

"You don't have to like it. You just do it. In a way you're lucky. I'm paying you cash. If I wanted I could just tell you and you'd do it. You know that?"

I nodded.

"Tonight starts it. From now on you'll have somebody close by, see? In one pocket you'll carry a white handkerchief. If you gotta blow, use it. In the other one there'll be a red wiper. When you see him blow into that."

"That's all?"

"Just duck about then, kid," Phil Carboy said softly, "and maybe you'll get to spend that two grand. Try to use it for run-out money and you won't get past the bus station." He stared into his glass, looked up at Rocco expectantly and held it out for a refill. "Kid, let me tell you something. I'm an old hand in this racket. I can tell what a guy or a dame is like from a block away. You've been around. I can tell that. I'm giving you a break because you're the type who knows the score and will play on the right side. I don't have to warn you about anything, do I?"

"No. I got the pitch."

"Any questions?"

"Just one," I said. "Renzo wants me to finger Vetter too. He isn't putting out any two grand for it. He just wants it, see? Suppose he catches up with me? What then?"

Carboy shouldn't've hesitated. He shouldn't have let that momentary look come into his eyes because it told me everything I wanted to know. Renzo was bigger than the whole pack of them and they got the jumps just thinking about it. All by himself he held a fifty-one percent interest and they were moving slowly when they bucked him. The little guy threw down the fresh drink with a quick motion of his hand and brought the smile back again. *In that second he had done a lot of thinking and spilled the answer straight out.* "We'll take care of Mark Renzo," he said. "Rocco, you and Lou take the kid home."

So I went out to the car and we drove back to the slums again. In the rear the reflections from the headlights of another car showed and the killers in it would be waiting for me to show the red handkerchief Carboy had handed me. I didn't know them and unless I was on the ball every minute I'd never get to know them. But they'd always be there, shadows that had no substance until the red showed, then the ground would get sticky with an even brighter red and maybe some of it would be mine.

They let me out two blocks away. The other car didn't show at all and I didn't look for it. My feet made hollow sounds on the sidewalk, going faster and faster until I was running up the steps of the house and when I was inside I slammed the door and leaned against it, trying hard to stop the pain in my chest.

Three-fifteen, the clock said. It ticked monotonously in the stillness, trailing me upstairs to my room. I eased inside, shut the door and locked it, standing there in the darkness until my eyes could see things. Outside a truck clashed its gears as it pulled up the hill and off in the distance a horn sounded.

I listened to them; familiar sounds, my face tightening as a not-so-familiar sound echoed behind them. It was a soft thing, a whisper that came at regular intervals in a choked-up way. Then I knew it was a sob coming from the other room and I went back to the hall and knocked on Nick's door.

His feet hit the floor, stayed there and I could hear his breathing coming hard. "It's Joe — open up."

I heard the wheeze his breath made as he let it out. The bedsprings creaked, he fell once getting to the door and the bolt snapped back. I looked at the purple blotches on his face and the open cuts over his eyes and grabbed him before he fell again. "Nick! What happened to you?"

"I'm . . . okay." He steadied himself on me and I led him back to the bed. "You got . . . some friends, pal."

"Cut it out. What happened? Who ran you through? Damn it, who did it?"

Nick managed to show a smile. It wasn't much and it hurt, but he made it. "You . . . in pretty big trouble, Joe."

"Pretty big."

"I didn't say nothing. They were here . . . asking questions. They didn't . . . believe what I told them, I guess. They sure laced me."

"The miserable slobs! You recognize them?"

His smile got sort of twisted and he nodded his head. "Sure, Joe . . . I know 'em. The fat one sat in . . . the car while they did it." His mouth clamped together hard. "It hurt . . . brother, it hurt!"

"Look," I said. "We're . . ."

"Nothing doing. I got enough. I don't want no more. Maybe they figured it's enough. That Renzo feller . . . he got hard boys around. See what they did, Joe? One . . . used a gun on me. You shoulda stood with Gordon, Joe. What the hell got into you to mess with them guys?"

"It wasn't me, Nick. Something came up. We can square it. I'll nail that fat slob if it's the last thing I do."

"It'll be the last thing. They gimme a message for you, pal. You're to stick around, see? You get seen with any other big boys in this town . . . and that's all. You know?"

"I know. Renzo told me that himself. He
didn't have to go through you."

"Joe . . ."

"Yeah?"

"He said for you to take a good look . . . at
me. I'm an example. A little one. He says to do
what he told you."

"He knows what he can do."

"Joe . . . for me. Lay off, huh? I don't feel so
good. Now I can't work for a while."

I patted his arm, fished a hundred buck bill
out of my pocket and squeezed it into his hand.
"Don't worry about it," I told him.

He looked at the bill unbelievingly, then at
me.

"Dough can't pay for . . . this, Joe. Kind of . . .
stay away from me . . . for awhile anyway,
okay?" He smiled again, lamely this time.
"Thanks for the C anyway. We been pretty good
buddies, huh?"

"Sure, Nick."

"Later we'll be again. Lemme knock off now.
You take it easy." His hands came up to his face
and covered it. I could hear the sobs starting
again and cursed the whole damn system up
and down and Renzo in particular. I swore at
the filth men like to wade in and the things they
do to other men. When I was done I got up off
the bed and walked to the door.

Behind me Nick said, "Joey . . ."

"Right here."

"Something's crazy in this town. Stories are going around . . . there's gonna be a lot of trouble. Everybody is after . . . you. You'll . . . be careful?"

"Sure." I opened the door, shut it softly and went back to my room. I stripped off my clothes and lay down in the bed, my mind turning over fast until I had it straightened out, then I closed my eyes and fell asleep.

My landlady waited until a quarter to twelve before she gave it the business on my door. She didn't do it like she usually did it. No jarring smashes against the panels, just a light tapping that grew louder until I said, "Yeah?"

"Mrs. Stacey, Joe. You think you should get up? A man is downstairs to see you."

"What kind of a man?"

This time the knob twisted slowly and the door opened a crack. Her voice was a harsh whisper that sounded nervous. "He's got on old clothes and a city water truck is parked outside. He didn't come to look at my water."

I grinned at that one. "I'll be right down," I said. I splashed water over my face, shaved it close and worked the adhesive off the bridge of my nose. It was swollen on one side, the blue running down to my mouth. One eye was smudged with purple.

Before I pulled on my jacket I stuffed the wad of dough into the lining through the tear in the sleeve, then I took a look in Nick's room. There were traces of blood on his pillow and the place was pretty upset, but Nick had managed to get out somehow for a day's work.

The guy in the chair sitting by the window was short and wiry looking. There was dirt under his fingernails and a stubble on his chin. He had a couple of small wrenches in a leather holster on his belt that bulged his coat out but the stuff was pure camouflage. There was a gun further back and I saw the same thing Mrs. Stacey saw. The guy was pure copper with badges for eyes.

He looked at me, nodded and said, "Joe Boyle?"

"Suppose I said no?" I sat down opposite him with a grin that said I knew all about it and though I knew he got it nothing registered at all.

"Captain Gerot tells me you'll cooperate. That true?"

There was a laugh in his eyes, an attitude of being deliberately polite when he didn't have to be. "Why?" I asked him. "Everybody seems to think I'm pretty hot stuff all of a sudden."

"You are, junior, you are. You're the only guy who can put his finger on a million dollar baby that we want bad. So you'll cooperate."

"Like a good citizen?" I made it sound the same as he did. "How much rides on Vetter and how much do I get?"

The sarcasm in his eyes turned to a nasty sneer. "Thousands ride, junior . . . and you don't get any. You just cooperate. Too many cops have worked too damn long on Vetter to let a crummy kid cut into the cake. *Now I'll tell you why you'll cooperate. There's a dame, see? Helen Troy. There's ways of slapping that tomato with a fat conviction for various reasons and unless you want to see her slapped, you'll cooperate. Catch now?"*

I called him something that fitted him right down to his shoes. He didn't lose a bit of that grin at all. "Catch something else," he said. "Get smart and I'll make your other playmates look like school kids. I like tough guys. I have fun working 'em over because that's what they understand. What there is to know I know. Take last night for instance. The boys paid you off for a finger job. Mark Renzo pays but in his own way. Now I'm setting up a deal. Hell, you don't have to take it . . . you can do what you please. Three people are dickering for what you know. I'm the only one who can hit where it really hurts.

"Think it over, Joey boy. Think hard but do it fast. I'll be waiting for a call from you and wherever you are, I'll know about it. I get impatient sometimes, so let's hear from you soon. Maybe if you take too long I'll prod you a little bit." He got up, stretched and wiped his eyes like he was tired. "Just ask for Detective Sergeant Gonzales," he said. "That's me."

The cop patted the tools on his belt and stood by the door. I said, "It's stinking to be a little man, isn't it? You got to keep making up for it."

There was pure, cold hate in his eyes for an answer. He gave me a long look that a snake would give a rabbit when he isn't too hungry yet. A look that said wait a little while, feller. Wait until I'm real hungry.

I watched the car pull away, then sat there at the window looking at the street. I had to wait almost an hour before I spotted the first, then picked up the second one ten minutes later. If there were more I didn't see them. I went back to the kitchen and took a look through the curtains at the blank behinds of the warehouses across the alley. Mrs. Stacey didn't say anything. She sat there with her coffee, making clicking noises with her false teeth.

I said, "Somebody washed the windows upstairs in the wholesale house."

"A man. Early this morning."

"They haven't been washed since I've been

here."

"Not for two years."

I turned around and she was looking at me as if something had scared her to death. *"How much are they paying you?" I said.*

She couldn't keep that greedy look out of her face even with all the phony indignation she tried to put on. Her mouth opened to say something when the phone rang and gave her the chance to cover up. She came back a few seconds later and said, "It's for you. Some man."

Then she stood there by the door where she always stood whenever somebody was on the phone. I said, "Joe Boyle speaking," and that was all. I let the other one speak his few words and when he was done I hung up.

I felt it starting to burn in me. A nasty feeling that makes you want to slam something. Nobody asked me . . . they just told and I was supposed to jump. I was the low man on the totem pole, a lousy kid who happened to fit into things . . . just the right size to get pushed around.

Vetter, I kept saying to myself. They were all scared to death of Vetter. The guy had something they couldn't touch. He was tough. He was smart. He was moving in for a kill and if ever one was needed it was needed now. They were all after him and no matter how many people who didn't belong there stood in the way their bullets would go right through them to reach Vetter. Yeah, they wanted him bad. So bad they'd kill each other to make sure he died too.

Well, the whole pack of 'em knew what they could do.

I pulled my jacket on and got outside. I went up the corner, grabbed a downtown bus and sat there without bothering to look around. At Third and Main I hopped off, ducked into a cafeteria and had a combination lunch. I let Mrs. Stacey get her calls in, gave them time to keep me well under cover, then flagged down a roving cab and gave the driver Helen's address. On the way over I looked out the back window for the second time and the light blue Chevvy was still in place, two cars behind and trailing steadily. In a way it didn't bother me if the boys inside were smart enough to check the black Caddie that rode behind it again.

I tapped the cabbie a block away, told him to let me out on the corner and paid him off. There wasn't a parking place along the street so the laddies in the cars were either going to cruise or double park, but it would keep them moving around so I could see what they were like anyway.

When I punched the bell I had to wait a full

minute before the lobby door clicked open. I went up the stairs, jolted the apartment door a few times and walked right into those beautiful eyes that were even prettier than the last time because they were worried first, then relieved when they saw me. She grabbed my arm and gave me that quick grin then pulled me inside and stood with her back to the door.

"Joe, Joe, you little jughead," she laughed. "You had me scared silly. Don't do anything like that again."

"Had to Helen. I wasn't going to come back but I had to do that too."

Maybe it was the way I said it that made her frown. "You're a funny kid."

"Don't say that."

Something changed in her eyes. "No. Maybe I shouldn't, should I?" She looked at me hard, her eyes soft, but piercing. "I feel funny when I look at you. I don't know why. Sometimes I've thought it was because I had a brother who was always in trouble. Always getting hurt. I used to worry about him too."

"What happened to him?"

"He was killed on the Anzio beachhead."

"Sorry."

She shook her head. "He didn't join the army because he was patriotic. He and another kid held up a joint. The owner was shot. He was dead by the time they found out who did it."

"You've been running all your life too, haven't you?"

The eyes dropped a second. "You could put it that way."

"What ties you here?"

"Guess."

"If you had the dough you'd beat it? Some place where nobody knew you?"

She laughed, a short jerky laugh. It was answer enough. I reached in the jacket, got out the pack of bills and flipped off a couple for myself.

I shoved the rest in her hand before she knew what it was. "Get going. Don't even bother to pack. Just move out of here and keep moving."

Her eyes were big and wide with an incredulous sort of wonder, then slightly misty when they came back to mine and she shook her head a little bit and said, "Joe . . . why? Why?"

"It would sound silly if I said it."

"Say it."

"When I'm all grown up I'll tell you maybe."

"Now."

I could feel the ache starting in me and my tongue didn't want to move, but I said, "Sometimes even a kid can feel pretty hard about a woman. Sad, isn't it?"

Helen said, "Joe," softly and had my face in her hands and her mouth was a hot torch that played against mine with a crazy kind of fierceness and it was all I could do to keep from grabbing her instead of pushing her away. My hands squeezed her hard, then I yanked the door open and got out of there. Behind me there was a sob and I heard my name said again, softly.

I ran the rest of the way down with my face all screwed up tight.

The blue Chevvy was down the street on the other side. It seemed to be empty and I didn't bother to poke around it. All I wanted was for whoever followed me to follow me away from there. So I gave it the full treatment. I made it look great. To them I must have seemed pretty jumpy and on my way to see somebody important. It took a full hour to reach THE CLIPPER that way and the only important one around was Bucky Edwards and he wasn't drunk this time.

He nodded, said, "Beer?" and when I shook my head, called down the bar for a tall orange. "Figured you'd be in sooner or later."

"Yeah?"

That wise old face wrinkled a little. "How does it feel to be live bait, kiddo?"

"You got big ears, grandma."

"I get around." He toasted his beer against my orange, put it down and said, "You're in pretty big trouble, Joe. Maybe you don't know it."

"I know it."

"You don't know how big. You haven't been here that long. Those boys put on the big squeeze."

It was my turn to squint. His face was set as if he smelled something he didn't like and there was ice in his eyes. "How much do you know, Bucky?"

His shoulders made a quick shrug. "Phil Carboy didn't post the depot and the bus station for nothing. He's got cars cruising the highways too. Making sure, isn't he?"

He looked at me and I nodded.

"Renzo is kicking loose too. He's pulling the strings tight. The guys on his payroll are getting nervous but they can't do a thing. No, sir, not a thing. Like a war. Everybody's just waiting." The set mouth flashed me a quick grin. "You're the key, boy. *If there was a way out I'd tell you to take it.*"

"Suppose I went to the cops?"

"Gerot?" Bucky shook his head. "You'd get help as long as he could keep you in a cell. People'd like to see him dead too. He's got an awfully bad habit of being honest. Ask him to show you his scars someday. It wouldn't be so bad if he was just honest, but he's smart and mean as hell too."

I drank half the orange and set it down in the wet circle on the bar. "Funny how things work out. All because of Vetter. And he's here because of Jack Cooley."

"I was wondering when you were gonna get around to it, kid," Bucky said.

"What?"

He didn't look at me. "Who are you working for?"

I waited a pretty long time before he turned his head around. I let him look at my face another long time before I said anything. Then: "I was pushing a junk cart, friend. I was doing okay, too. I wasn't working for trouble. Now I'm getting pretty curious. In my own way I'm not so stupid, but now I want to find out the score. One way or another I'm finding out. So they paid me off but they aren't figuring on me spending much of that cabbage. After it's over I get chopped down and it starts all over again, whatever it is. That's what I'm finding out. Why I'm bait for whatever it is. Who do I see, Bucky? You're in the know. Where do I go to find out?"

"Cooley could have told you," he said quietly.

"Nuts. He's dead."

"Maybe he can still tell you."

My fingers were tight around the glass now. "The business about Cooley getting it because of the deal on Renzo's tables is out?"

"Might be."

"Talk straight unless you're scared silly of those punks too. Don't give me any puzzles if you know something."

Bucky's eyebrows went up, then down slowly over the grin in his eyes. "Talk may be cheap, son," he said, "but life comes pretty expensively." He nodded sagely and said, "I met Cooley in lotsa places. Places he shouldn't have been. He was a man looking around. He could have found something."

"Like what?"

"Like why we have gangs in this formerly peaceful city of ours. Why we have paid-for politicians and clambakes with some big faces showing. They're not eating clams . . they're talking."

"These places where you kept seeing Cooley . . ."

"River joints. Maybe he liked fish."

You could tell when Bucky was done talking. I went down to Main, found a show I hadn't seen and went in. There were a lot of things I wanted to think about.

Part Three

Vetter! This is the name hiding an unknown face—a name that has young Joe Boyle serving as decoy in a dangerous game of death.

AT ELEVEN-FIFTEEN the feature wound up and I started back outside. In the glass reflection of the lobby door I saw somebody behind me but I didn't look back. There could have been one more in the crowd that was around the entrance outside. Maybe two. Nobody seemed to pay any attention to me and I didn't care if they did or not.

I waited for a Main Street bus, took it down about a half mile, got off at the darkened supermarket and started up the road. You get the creeps in places like that. It was an area where some optimist had started a factory and ran it until the swamp crept in. When the footings gave and the walls cracked, they moved out, and now the black skeletons of the buildings were all that were left, with gaping holes for eyes and a mouth that seemed to breathe out a fetid swamp odor. But there were still people there. The dozen or so company houses that were propped against the invading swamp showed dull yellow lights, and the garbage smell of unwanted humanity fought the swamp odor. You could hear them, too, knowing that they watched you from the shadows of their porches. You could feel them stirring in their jungle shacks and catch the pungency of the alcohol they brewed out of anything they could find.

There was a low moan of a train from the south side and its single eye picked out the trestle across the bay and followed it. The freight lumbered up, slowed for the curve that ran through the swamps and I heard the bindle stiffs yelling as they hopped off, looking for the single hard topped road that took them to their quarters for the night.

The circus sign was on the board fence. In the darkness it was nothing but a bleached white square, but when I lit a cigarette I could see the faint orange impressions that used to be supposedly wild animals. The match went out and I lit another, got the smoke fired up and stood there a minute in the dark.

The voice was low. A soft, quiet voice more inaudible than a whisper. "One is back at the corner. There's another a hundred feet down."

"I know," I said.

"You got nerve."

"Let's not kid me. I got your message. Sorry I had to cut it short, but a pair of paid-for ears were listening in."

"Sorry Renzo gave you a hard time."

"So am I. The others did better by me."

Somebody coughed down the road and I flattened against the boards away from the white sign. It came again, further away this time and I felt better. I said, "What gives?"

"You had a cop at your place this morning."

"I spotted him."

"There's a regular parade behind you." *A pause, then,* "What did you tell them?"

I dragged in on the smoke, watched it curl up against the fence. "I told them he was big. Tough. I didn't see his face too well. What did you expect me to tell them?"

I had a feeling like he smiled.

"They aren't happy," *he said.*

I grinned too. "Vetter. They hate the name. It scares them." *I pulled on the butt again.* "It scares me too when I think of it too much."

"You don't have anything to worry about."

"Thanks."

"Keep playing it smart. You know what they're after?"

I nodded, even though he couldn't see me. "Cooley comes into it someplace. It was something he knew."

"Smart lad. I knew you were a smart lad the first time 1 saw you. Yes, it was Cooley."

"Who was he?" I asked.

Nothing for a moment. I could hear him breathing and his feet moved but that was all. The red light on the tail of the caboose winked at me and 1 knew it would have to be short.

"An adventurer, son. A romantic adventurer who went where the hunting was profitable and the odds long. He liked long odds. He found how they were slipping narcotics in through a new door and tapped them for a sweet haul. They say four million. It was a paid-for shipment and he got away with it. Now the boys have to make good."

The caboose was almost past now. He said, "I'll call you if I want you."

I flipped the butt away, watching it bounce sparks across the dirt. I went on a little bit further where I could watch the fires from the jungles and when I had enough of it I started back.

At the tree the guy who had been waiting there said, "You weren't thinking of hopping that freight, were you, kid"

I didn't jump like I was supposed to. I said, "When I want to leave, I'll leave."

"Be sure to tell Mr. Carboy first, huh?"

"I'll tell him," I said.

He stayed there, not following me. I passed the buildings again, then felt better when I saw the single street light on the corner of Main. There was nobody there that I could see, but that didn't count. He was around someplace.

I had to wait ten minutes for a bus. It seemed longer than it was. I stayed drenched in the yellow light and thought of the voice behind the fence and what it had to say. When the bus pulled up I got on, stayed there until I reached the lights again and got off. By that time a lot of things were making sense, falling into a recognizable pattern. I walked down the street to an all night drug store, had a drink at the counter then went back to the phone booth.

I dialed the police number and asked for Gonzales, Sergeant Gonzales. There was a series of clicks as the call was switched and the cop said, "Gonzales speaking."

"This is Joe, copper. Remember me?"

"Don't get too fresh, sonny," he said. His voice had a knife in it.

"Phil Carboy paid me some big money to finger Vetter. He's got men tailing me."

His pencil kept up a steady tapping against the side of the phone. Finally he said, "I was wondering when you'd call it in. You were real lucky, Joe. For a while I thought I was going to have to persuade you a little to cooperate. You were real lucky. Keep me posted."

I heard the click in my ear as he hung up and I spat out the things into the dead phone I felt like telling him to his face. Then I fished out another coin, dropped it in and dialed the same number. This time I asked for Captain Gerot. The guy at the switchboard said he had left about six but that he could probably be reached at his club. He gave me the number and I checked it through. The attendant who answered said he had left about an hour ago but would probably call back to see if there were any messages for him and were there? I told him to get the number so I could put the call through myself and hung up.

It took me a little longer to find Bucky Edwards. He had stewed in his own juices too long and he was almost all gone. I said, "Bucky, I need something bad. I want Jack Cooley's last address. You remember that much?"

He hummed a little bit. "Rooming house. Between Wells and Capitol. It's all white, Joe. Only white house."

"Thanks, Bucky."

"You in trouble, Joe?"

"Not yet."

"You will be. Now you will be." That was all. He put the phone back so easily I didn't hear it go. Damn, I thought, he knows the score but he won't talk. He's got all the scoop and he clams up.

I had another drink at the counter, picked up a deck of smokes and stood outside while I lit one. The street was quieting down. Both curbs were lined with parked heaps, dead things that rested until morning when they'd be whipped alive again.

Not all of them though. I was sure of that. I thought I caught a movement across the street in a doorway. It was hard to tell. I turned north and walked fast until I reached Benson Road, then cut down it to the used car lot.

Now was when they'd have a hard time. Now was when they were playing games in my back yard and if they didn't know every inch of the way somebody was going to get hurt. They weren't kids, these guys. They had played the game themselves and they'd know all the angles. Almost all, anyway. They'd know when I tried to get out of the noose and as soon as they did, they'd quit playing and start working. They wouldn't break their necks sticking to a trail when they could bottle me up.

All I had to do was keep them from knowing for a while.

I crossed the lot, cutting through the parked cars, picked up the alley going back of the houses and stuck to the hedgerows until I was well down it. By that time I had a lead. If I looked back I'd spoil it so I didn't look back. I picked up another block at the fork in the alley, standing deliberately under the lone light at the end, not hurrying, so they could see me. I made it seem as though I were trying to pick out one of the houses in the darkness, and when I made up my mind, went through the gate in the fence.

After that I hurried. I picked up the short-cuts, made the street and crossed it between lights. I reached Main again, grabbed a cruising cab in the middle of the block, had him haul me across town to the docks and got out. It took fifteen minutes longer to reach the white house Bucky told me about. I grinned to myself and wondered if the boys were still watching the place they thought I went into. Maybe it would be a little while before they figured the thing out.

It would be time enough.

The guy who answered the door was all wrapped up in a bathrobe, his hair stringing down his face. He squinted at me, reluctant to be polite, but not naturally tough enough to be anything else but. He said, "If you're looking for a room you'll have to come around in the morning. I'm sorry."

I showed him a bill with two numbers on it.

"Well. . ."

"I don't want a room."

He looked at the bill again, then a quick flash of terror crossed his face. His eyes rounded open, looked at me hard, then dissolved into curiosity. "Come . . . in."

The door closed and he stepped around me into a small sitting room and snapped on a shaded desk lamp. His eyes went back down to the bill. I handed it over and watched it disappear into the bathrobe. "Yes?"

"Jack Cooley."

The words did something to his face. It showed terror again, but not as much as before.

"I really don't . . ."

"Forget the act. I'm not working for anybody in town. I was a friend of his."

This time he scowled, not believing me.

I said, "Maybe I don't look it, but I was."

"So? What is it you want?" He licked his lips, seemed to tune his ears for some sound from upstairs. "Everybody's been here. Police, newspapers. Those . . . men from town. They all want something."

"Did Jack leave anything behind?"

"Sure. Clothes, letters, the usual junk. The police have all that."

"Did you get to see any of it?"

"Well . . . the letters were from dames. Nothing important."

I nodded, fished around for a question a second before I found one. "How about his habits?"

The guy shrugged. "He paid on time. Usually came in late and slept late. No dames in his room."

"That's all?"

He was getting edgy. "What else is there? I didn't go out with the guy. So now I know he spent plenty of nights in Renzo's joint. I hear talk. You want to know what kind of butts he smoked? Hobbies, maybe? Hell, what is there to tell? He goes out at night. Sometimes he goes fishing. Sometimes . . ."

"Where?" I interrupted.

"Where what?"

"Fishing."

"On one of his boats. He borrowed my stuff. He was fishing the day before he got bumped. Sometimes he'd slip me a ticket and I'd get away from the old lady."

"How do the boats operate?"

He shrugged again, pursing his mouth.

"They go down the bay to the tip of the inlet, gas up, pick up beer at Gulley's and go about ten miles out. Coming back they stop at Gulley's for more beer and for the guys to dump the fish they don't want. Gulley sells it in town. Everybody is usually drunk and happy." He gave me another thoughtful look. "You writing a book about your friend?" he said sarcastically.

"Could be. Could be. I hate to see him dead."

"If you ask me, he never should've fooled around Renzo. You better go home and save your money from now on, sonny."

"I'll take your advice," I said, "and be handyman around a rooming house."

He gave me a dull stare as I stood up and didn't bother to go to the door with me. He still had his hand in his pocket wrapped around the bill I gave him.

The street was empty and dark enough to keep me wrapped in a blanket of shadows. I stayed close to the houses, stopping now and then to listen. When I was sure I was by myself I felt better and followed the water smell of the bay.

At River Road a single pump gas station showed lights and the guy inside sat with his feet propped up on the desk. He opened one eye when I walked in, gave me the change I wanted for the phone, then went back to sleep again. I dialed the number of Gerot's club, got the attendant and told him what I wanted. He gave me another number and I punched it out on the dial.

Two persons answered before a voice said, "Gerot speaking."

"Hello, Captain. This is Joe. I was. . ."

"I remember," he said.

"I called Sergeant Gonzales tonight. Phil Carboy paid me off to finger Vetter. Now I got two parties pushing me."

"Three. Don't forget us."

"I'm not forgetting."

"I hear you've been moving around, Joe. Those parties are excited. Where are you?"

I didn't think he'd bother to trace the call, so I said, "Some joint in town."

His voice sounded light this time. "About Vetter. Tell me."

"Nothing to tell."

"You had a call this morning." I felt the chills starting to run up my back. They had a tap on my line already. "The voice wasn't familiar and it said some peculiar things."

"I know. I didn't get it. I thought it was part of Renzo's outfit getting wise. They beat up a buddy of mine so I'd know what a real beat-up guy looks like. It was all double talk to me."

He was thinking it over. When he was ready

he said, "Maybe so, kid. You hear about that dame you were with?"

I could hardly get the words out of my mouth. "Helen? No . . . What?"

"Somebody shot at her. Twice."

"Did . . ."

"Not this time. She was able to walk away from it this time."

"Who was it? Who shot at her?"

"That, little chum, is something we'd like to know too. She was waiting for a train out of town. The next time maybe we'll have better luck. There'll be a next time, in case you're interested."

"Yeah, I'm interested . . . and thanks. You know where she is now?"

"No, but we're looking around. *I hope we can find her first.*"

I put the phone back and tried to get the dry taste out of my mouth. When I thought I could talk again I dialed Helen's apartment, hung on while the phone rang endlessly, then held the receiver fork down until I got my coin back. I had to get Renzo's club number from the book and the gravelly voice that answered rasped that the feature attraction hadn't put in an appearance that night and for something's sake to cut off the chatter and wait until tomorrow because the club was closed.

So I stood there and said things to myself until I was all balled up into a knot. I could see the parade of faces I hated drifting past my mind and all I could think of was how bad I wanted to smash every one of them as they came by. Helen had tried to run for it. She didn't get far. Now where could she be? Where does a beautiful blonde go who is trying to hide? Who would take her in if they knew the score?

I could feel the sweat starting on my neck, soaking the back of my shirt. All of a sudden I felt washed out and wrung dry. Gone. All the way gone. Like there wasn't anything left of me any more except a big hate for a whole damn city, the mugs who ran it and the people who were afraid of the mugs. And it wasn't just one city either. There would be more of them scattered all over the states. For the people, by the people, Lincoln had said. Yeah. Great.

I turned around and walked out. I didn't even bother to look back and if they were there, let them come. I walked for a half hour, found a cab parked at a corner with the driver sacking it behind the wheel and woke him up. I gave him the boarding house address and climbed in the back.

He let me off at the corner, collected his dough and turned around.

Then I heard that voice again and I froze the

butt halfway to my mouth and squashed the matches in the palm of my hand.

It said, "Go ahead and light it."

I breathed that first drag out with the words, "You nuts? They're all around this place."

"I know. Now be still and listen. The dame knows the score. They tried for her .. ."

We heard the feet at the same time. They were light as a cat, fast. Then he came out of the darkness and all I could see was the glint of the knife in his hand and the yell that was in my throat choked off when his fingers bit into my flesh. I had time to see that same hardened face that had looked into mine not so long ago, catch an expressionless grin from the hard boy, then the other shadows opened and the side of a palm smashed down against his neck. He pitched forward with his head at a queer, stiff angle, his mouth wrenched open and I knew it was only a reflex that kept it that way because the hard boy was dead. You could hear the knife chatter across the sidewalk and the sound of the body hitting, a sound that really wasn't much yet was a thunderous crash that split the night wide open.

The shadows the hand had reached out from seemed to open and close again, and for a short second I was alone. Just a short second. I heard the whisper that was said too loud. The snick of a gun somewhere, then I closed in against the building and ran for it.

At the third house I faded into the alley and listened. Back there I could hear them talking, then a car started up down the street. I cut around behind the houses, found the fences and stuck with them until I was at my place, then snaked into the cellar door.

When I got upstairs I slipped into the hall and reached for the phone. I asked for the police and got them. All I said was that somebody was being killed and gave the address. Then I grinned at the darkness, hung up without giving my name and went upstairs to my room. From way across town a siren wailed a lonely note, coming closer little by little. It was a pleasant sound at that. It would give my friend from the shadows plenty of warning too. He was quite a guy. Strong. Whoever owned the dead man was going to walk easy with Vetter after this.

I walked into my room, closed the door and was reaching for the bolt when the chair moved in the corner. Then she said, "Hello, Joe," and the air in my lungs hissed out slowly between my teeth.

I said, "Helen." I don't know which one of us moved. I like to think it was her. But suddenly she was there in my arms with her face buried in my shoulder, stifled sobs pouring out of her body while I tried to tell her that it was all right.

Her body was pressed against me, a fire that seemed to dance as she trembled, fighting to stay close to me.

"Helen, Helen, take it easy. Nothing will hurt you now. You're okay." I lifted her head away and smoothed back her hair. "Listen, you're all right here."

Her mouth was too close. Her eyes were too wet and my mind was thinking things that didn't belong there. My arms closed tighter and I found her mouth, warm and soft, a salty sweetness that clung desperately and talked to me soundlessly. But it stopped the trembling and when she pulled away she smiled and said my name softly.

"How'd you get here, Helen?"

Her smile tightened. "I was brought up in a place like this a long time ago. There are always ways. I found one."

"I heard what happened. Who was it?"

She tightened under my hands. "I don't know. I was waiting for a train when it happened. I just ran after that. When I got out on the street, it happened again."

"No cops?"

She shook her head. "Too fast. I kept running."

"They know it was you?"

"I was recognized in the station. Two men

there had caught my show and said hello. You know how. They could have said something."

I could feel my eyes starting to squint. "Don't be so damn calm about it."

The tight smile twisted up at the corner. It was like she was reading my mind. She seemed to soften a moment and I felt her fingers brush my face. "I told you I wasn't like other girls, Joe. Not like the kind of girl you should know. Let's say it's all something I've seen before. After a bit you get used to it."

"Helen . . ."

"I'm sorry, Joe."

I shook my head slowly. "No . . . I'm the one who's sorry. People like you should never get like that. Not you."

"Thanks." She looked at me, something strange in her eyes that I could see even in the half light of the room. And this time it happened slowly, the way it should be. The fire was close again, and real this time, very real. Fire that could have burned deeply if the siren hadn't closed in and stopped outside.

I pushed her away and went to the window. The beams of the flashlights traced paths up the sidewalk. The two cops were cursing the cranks in the neighborhood until one stopped, grunted something and picked up a sliver of steel that lay by the curb. But there was nothing else.

Then they got back in the cruiser and drove off.

Helen said, "What was it?"

"There was a dead man out there. Tomorrow there'll be some fun."

"Joe!"

"Don't worry about it. At least we know how we stand. It was one of their boys. He made a pass at me on the street and got taken."

"You do it?"

I shook my head. "Not me. A guy. A real big guy with hands that can kill."

"Vetter." She said it breathlessly.

I shrugged.

Her voice was a whisper. "I hope he kills them all. Every one." Her hand touched my arm. "Somebody tried to kill Renzo earlier. They got one of his boys." Her teeth bit into her lip. "There were two of them so it wasn't Vetter. You know what that means?"

I nodded. "War. They want Renzo dead to get Vetter out of town. They don't want him around or he'll move into their racket sure."

"He already has." I looked at her sharply and she nodded. "I saw one of the boys in the band. Renzo's special car was hijacked as it was leaving the city. Renzo claimed they got nothing but he's pretty upset. I heard other things too. The whole town's tight."

"Where do you come in, Helen?"

"What?" Her voice seemed taut.

"You. Let's say you and Cooley. What string are you pulling?" Her hand left my arm and hung down at her side. If I'd slapped her she would have had the same expression on her face. I said, "I'm sorry. I didn't mean it like that. You liked Jack Cooley pretty well, didn't you?"

"Yes." She said it quietly.

"You told me what he was like once. What was he really like?" The hurt flashed in her face again. "Like them," she said. "Gay, charming, but like them. He wanted the same things. He just went after them differently, that's all."

"The guy I saw tonight said you know things."

Her breath caught a little bit. "I didn't know before, Joe."

"Tell me."

"When I packed to leave . . . then I found out. Jack . . . left certain things with me. One was an envelope. There were cancelled checks in it for thousands of dollars made out to Renzo. The one who wrote the checks is a racketeer in New York. There was a note pad too with dates and amounts that Renzo paid Cooley."

"Blackmail."

"I think so. What was more important was what was in the box he left with me. *Heroin.*"

I swung around slowly. "Where is it?"

"Down a sewer. I've seen what the stuff can

do to a person."

"Much of it?

"Maybe a quarter pound."

"We could have had him," I said. "We could have had him and you dumped the stuff!"

Her hand touched me again. "No . . . there wasn't that much of it. Don't you see, it's bigger than that. What Jack had was only a sample. Some place there's more of it, much more."

"Yeah," I said. I was beginning to see things now. They were starting to straighten themselves out and it made a pattern. The only trouble was that the pattern was so simple it didn't begin to look real.

"Tomorrow we start," I said. "We work by night. Roll into the sack and get some sleep. If I can keep the landlady out of here we'll be okay. You sure nobody saw you come in?"

"Nobody saw me."

"Good. Then they'll only be looking for me."

"Where will you sleep?"

I grinned at her. "In the chair."

I heard the bed creak as she eased back on it, then I slid into the chair. After a long time she said, "Who are you, Joe?"

I grunted something and closed my eyes. I wished I knew myself sometimes.

Part Four

The cards are on the table as Joe Boyle fights his way to the end of the line. And waiting there with murder in his fist—Vetter!

I WOKE UP just past noon. Helen was still asleep, restlessly tossing in some dream. The sheet had slipped down to her waist, and everytime she moved, her body rippled with sinuous grace. I stood looking at her for a long time, my eyes devouring her, every muscle in my body wanting her. There were other things to do, and I cursed those other things and set out to do them.

When I knew the landlady was gone I made a trip downstairs to her ice box and lifted enough for a quick meal. I had to wake Helen up to eat, then sat back with an old magazine to let the rest of the day pass by. At seven we made the first move. It was a nice simple little thing that put the whole neighborhood in an uproar for a half hour but gave us a chance to get out without being spotted.

All I did was call the fire department and tell them there was a gas leak in one of the tenements. They did the rest. Besides holding everybody back from the area they evacuated a whole row of houses, including us and while they were trying to run down the false alarm we grabbed a cab and got out.

Helen asked, "Where to?"

"A place called Gulley's. It's a stop for the fishing boats. You know it?"

"I know it." She leaned back against the cushions. "It's a tough place to be. Jack took me out there a couple of times."

"He did? Why?"

"Oh, we ate, then he met some friends of his. We were there when the place was raided. Gulley was selling liquor after closing hours. Good thing Jack had a friend on the force."

"Who was that?"

"Some detective with a Mexican name."

"Gonzales," I said.

She looked at me. "That's right." She frowned slightly. "I didn't like him at all."

That was a new angle. One that didn't fit in. Jack with a friend on the force. I handed Helen a cigarette, lit it and sat back with mine.

It took a good hour to reach the place and at first glance it didn't seem worth the ride. From the highway the road weaved out onto a sand spit and in the shadows you could see the parked cars and occasionally couples in them. Here and there along the road the lights of the car picked up the glint of beer cans and empty bottles. I gave the cabbie an extra five and told him to wait and when we went down the gravel path, he pulled it under the trees and switched off his lights.

Gulley's was a huge shack built on the sand with a porch extending out over the water. There wasn't a speck of paint on the weather-racked framework and over the whole place the smell of fish hung like a blanket. It looked like a creep joint until you turned the corner and got a peek at the nice modern dock setup he had and the new addition on the side that probably made the place the yacht club's slumming section. If it didn't have anything else it had atmosphere. We were right on the tip of the peninsular that jutted out from the mainland and like the sign said, it was the last chance for the boats to fill up with the bottled stuff before heading out to deep water.

I told Helen to stick in the shadows of the hedge row that ran around the place while I took a look around, and though she didn't like it, she melted back into the brush. I could see a couple of figures on the porch, but they were talking too low for me to hear what was going on. Behind the bar that ran across the main room inside, a flat-faced fat guy leaned over reading the paper with his ears pinned inside a headset. Twice he reached back, frowning and fiddled with a radio under the counter. When the phone rang he scowled again, slipped off the headset and said, "Gulley speaking. Yeah. Okay. So-long."

When he went back to his paper I crouched down under the rows of windows and eased around the side. The sand was a thick carpet that silenced all noise and the gentle lapping of the water against the docks covered any other racket I could make. I was glad to have it that way too. There were guys spotted around the place that you couldn't see until you looked hard and they were just lounging. Two were by the building and the other two at the foot of the docks, edgy birds who lit occasional cigarettes and shifted around as they smoked them. One of them said something and a pair of them swung around to watch the twin beams of a car coming up the highway. I looked too, saw them turn in a long arc then cut straight for the shack.

One of the boys started walking my way, his

feet squeaking in the dry sand. I dropped back around the corner of the building, watched while he pulled a bottle out from under the brush, then started back the way I had come.

The car door slammed. A pair of voices mixed in an argument and another one cut them off. When I heard it I could feel my lips peel back and I knew that if I had a knife in my fist and Mark Renzo passed by me in the dark, whatever he had for supper would spill all over the ground. There was another voice, swearing at something. Johnny. Nice, gentle Johnny who was going to cripple me for life.

I wasn't worrying about Helen because she wouldn't be sticking her neck out. I was hoping hard that my cabbie wasn't reading any paper by his dome light and when I heard the boys reach the porch and go in, I let my breath out hardly realizing that my chest hurt from holding it in so long.

You could hear their hellos from inside, muffled sounds that were barely audible. I had maybe a minute to do what I had to do and didn't waste any time doing it. I scuttled back under the window that was at one end of the bar, had time to see Gulley shaking hands with Renzo over by the door, watched him close and lock it and while they were still far enough away not to notice the movement, slid the window up an inch and flattened against the wall.

They did what I expected they'd do. I heard Gulley invite them to the bar for a drink and set out the glasses. Renzo said, "Good stuff."

"Only the best. You know that."

Johnny said, "Sure. You treat your best customers right."

Bottle and glasses clinked again for another round. Then the headset that was under the bar started clicking. I took a quick look, watched Gulley pick it up, slap one earpiece against his head and jot something down on a pad.

Renzo said, "She getting in without trouble?"

Gulley set the headset down and leaned across the bar. He looked soft, but he'd been around a long time and not even Renzo was playing any games with him. "Look," he said, "You got your end of the racket. Keep out of mine. You know?"

"Getting tough, Gulley?"

I could almost hear Gulley smile. "Yeah. Yeah, in case you want to know. You damn well better blow off to them city lads, not me."

"Ease off," Renzo told him. He didn't sound rough any more. "Heard a load was due in tonight."

"You hear too damn much."

"It didn't come easy. I put out a bundle for the information. You know why?" Gulley didn't say anything. Renzo said, "I'll tell you why. I need that stuff. You know why?"

"Tough. Too bad. You know. What you want is already paid for and is being delivered. You ought to get your head out of your whoosis."

"Gulley . . ." Johnny said really quiet. "We ain't kidding. We need that stuff. The big boys are getting jumpy. They think we pulled a fast one. They don't like it. They don't like it so bad maybe they'll send a crew down here to straighten everything out and you may get straightened too."

Inside Gulley's feet were nervous on the floorboards. He passed in front of me once, his hands busy wiping glasses. "You guys are nuts. Carboy paid for this load. So I should stand in the middle?"

"Maybe it's better than standing in front of us," Johnny said.

"You got rocks. Phil's out of the local stuff now. He's got a pretty big outfit."

"Just peanuts, Gulley, just peanuts."

"Not any more. He's moving in since you dumped the big deal."

Gulley's feet stopped moving. His voice had a whisper in it. "So you were big once. Now I see you sliding. The big boys are going for bargains and they don't like who can't deliver, especially when it's been paid for. That was one big load. It was special. So you dumped it. Phil's smart enough to pick it up from there and now he may be top dog. I'm not in the middle. Not without an answer to Phil and he'll need a good one."

"Vetter's in town, Gulley!" Renzo almost spat the word out. "You know how he is? He ain't a gang you bust up. He's got a nasty habit of killing people. Like always, he's moving in. So we pay you for the stuff and deliver what we lost. We make it look good and you tell Phil it was Vetter. He'll believe that."

I could hear Gulley breathing hard. "Jerks, you guys," he said. There was a hiss in his words. "I should string it on Vetter. Man, you're plain nuts. I seen that guy operate before. Who the hell you think edged into that Frisco deal? Who got Morgan in El Paso while he was packing a half a million in cash and another half in powder. So a chowderhead hauls him in to cream some local fish and the guy walks away with the town. *Who the hell is that guy?"*

Johnny's laugh was bitter. Sharp. Gulley had said it all and it was like a knife sticking in and being twisted. "I'd like to meet him. Seems like he was a buddy of Jack Cooley. You remember Jack Cooley, Gulley? You were in on that. Cooley got off with your kick too. Maybe Vetter would like to know about that."

"Shut up."

"Not yet. We got business to talk about."

Gulley seemed out of breath. "Business be damned. I ain't tangling with Vetter."

"Scared?"

"Damn right, and so are you. So's everybody else."

"Okay," Johnny said. "So for one guy or a couple he's trouble. In a big town he can make his play and move fast. Thing is with enough guys in a burg like this he can get nailed."

"And how many guys get nailed with him. He's no dope. Who you trying to smoke?"

"Nuts, who cares who gets nailed as long as it ain't your own bunch. You think Phil Carboy'll go easy if he thinks Vetter jacked a load out from under him? Like you told us, Phil's an up and coming guy. He's growing. He figures on being the top kick around here and let Vetter give him the business and he goes all out to get the guy. So two birds are killed. Vetter and Carboy. Even if Carboy gets him, his load's gone. He's small peanuts again."

"Where does that get me?" Gulley asked.

"I was coming to that. You make yours. The percentage goes up ten. Good?"

Gulley must have been thinking greedy. He started moving again, his feet coming closer. He said, "You talk big. Where's the cabbage?"

"I got it on me," Renzo said. "You know what Phil was paying for the junk?"

"The word said two million."

"It's gonna cost to take care of the boys on the boat."

"Not so much." Renzo's laugh had no humor in it. "They talk and either Carbov'll finish 'em or Vetter will. They stay shut up for free."

"How much for me?" Gulley asked.

"One hundred thousand for swinging the deal, plus the extra percentage. You think it's worth it?"

"I'll go it," Gulley said.

Nobody spoke for a second, then Gulley said, "I'll phone the boat to pull into the slipside docks. They can unload there. The stuff is packed in beer cans. It won't make a big package so look around for it. They'll probably shove it under one of the benches."

"Who gets the dough?"

"You row out to the last boat mooring. The thing is red with a white stripe around it. Unscrew the top and drop it in."

"Same as the way we used to work it?"

"Right. The boys on the boat won't like going in the harbor and they'll be plenty careful, so don't stick around to lift the dough and the stuff too. That breed on the ship got a lockerfull of chatter guns he likes to hand out to his crew."

"It'll get played straight."

"I'm just telling you."

Renzo said, "What do you tell Phil?"

"You kidding? I don't say nothing. All I know is I lose contact with the boat. Next the word goes that Vetter is mixed up in it. I don't say nothing." He paused for a few seconds, his breath whistling in his throat, then, "But don't forget something . . . You take Carboy for a sucker and maybe even Vetter. Lay off me. I keep myself covered. Anything happens to me and the next day the cops get a letter naming names. Don't ever forget that."

Renzo must have wanted to say something. He didn't. Instead he rasped, "Go get the cash for this guy."

Somebody said, "Sure, boss," and walked across the room. I heard the lock snick open, then the door.

"This better work," Renzo said. He fiddled with his glass a while. "I'd sure like to know what that punk did with the other stuff."

"He ain't gonna sell it, that's for sure," Johnny told him. "You think maybe Cooley and Vetter were in business together."

"I'm thinking maybe Cooley was in business with a lot of people. That lousy blonde. When I get her she'll talk plenty. I should've kept my damn eyes open."

"I tried to tell you, boss."

"Shut up," Renzo said. "You just see that she gets found."

I didn't wait to hear any more. I got down in the darkness and headed back to the path. Overhead the sky was starting to lighten as the moon came up, a red circle that did funny things to the night and started the long fingers of shadows drifting out from the scraggly brush. The trees seemed to be ponderous things that reached down with sharp claws, feeling around in the breeze for something to grab. I found the place where I had left Helen, found a couple of pebbles and tossed them back into the brush. I heard her gasp, then whispered her name.

She came forward silently, said, "Joe?" in a hushed tone.

"Yeah. *Let's get out of here.*"

"What happened?"

"Later. I'll start back to the cab to make sure it's clear. If you don't hear anything, follow me. Got it?"

". . . yes." She was hesitant and I couldn't blame her. I got off the gravel path into the sand, took it easy and tried to search out the shadows. I reached the clearing, stood there until I was sure the place was empty then hopped over to the cab.

I had to shake the driver awake and he came

out of it stupidly. "Look, keep your lights off going back until you're on the highway, then keep 'em on low. There's enough moon to see by."

"Hey . . . I don't want trouble."

"You'll get it unless you do what I tell you."

"Well . . . okay."

"A dame's coming out in a minute. Soon as she comes start it up and try to keep it quiet."

I didn't have long to wait. I heard her feet on the gravel, walking fast but not hurrying. Then I heard something else that froze me a second. A long, low whistle of appreciation like the kind any blonde'll get from the pool hall boys. I hopped in the cab, held the door open. "Let's go, feller," I said.

As soon as the engine ticked over Helen started to run. I yanked her inside as the car started moving and kept down under the windows. She said, "Somebody . . ."

"I heard it."

"I didn't see who it was."

"Maybe it'll pass. Enough cars come out here to park."

Her hand was tight in mine, the nails biting into my palm. She was half-turned on the seat, her dress pulled back over the glossy knees of her nylons, her breasts pressed against my arm. She stayed that way until we reached the highway then little by little eased up until she was sitting back against the cushions. I tapped my forefinger against my lips then pointed to the driver. Helen nodded, smiled, then squeezed my hand again. This time it was different. The squeeze went with the smile.

I paid off the driver at the edge of town. He got more than the meter said, a lot more. It was big enough to keep a man's mouth shut long enough to get him in trouble when he opened it too late. When he was out of sight we walked until we found another cab, told the driver to get us to a small hotel someplace, and the usual leer and blonde inspection muttered the name of a joint and pulled away from the curb.

It was the kind of a place where they don't ask questions and don't believe what you write in the register anyway. I signed *Mr. and Mrs. Valiscivitch*, paid the bill in advance for a week and when the clerk read the name I got a screwy look because the name was too screwballed to be anything but real to him. Maybe he figured his clientele was changing. When we got to the room I said, "You park here for a few days."

"Are you going to tell me anything?"

"Should I?"

"You're strange, Joe. A very strange boy."

"Stop calling me a boy."

Her face got all beautiful again and when she

smiled there was a real grin in it. She stood there with her hands on her hips and her feet apart like she was going into some part of her routine and I could feel my body starting to burn at the sight of her. She could do things with herself by just breathing and she did them, the smile and her eyes getting deeper all the time. She saw what was happening to me and said, "You're not such a boy after all." She held out her hand and I took it, pulling her in close. "The first time you were a boy. All bloody, dirt ground into your face. When Renzo tore you apart I could have killed him. Nobody should do that to another one, especially a boy. But then there was Johnny and you seemed to grow up. I'll never forget what you did to him."

"He would have hurt you."

"You're even older now. Or should I say matured? I think you finished growing up last night, Joe, last night . . . with me. I saw you grow up, and I only hope I haven't hurt you in the process. I never was much good for anybody. That's why I left home, I guess. Everyone I was near seemed to get hurt. Even me."

"You're better than they are, Helen. The breaks were against you, that's all.

"Joe . . . do you know you're the first one who did anything nice for me without wanting . . . something?"

"Helen . . ."

"No, don't say anything. Just take a good look at me. See everything that I am? It shows. I know it shows. I was a lot of things that weren't nice. I'm the kind men want but who won't introduce to their families. I'm a beautiful piece of dirt, Joe." Her eyes were wet. I wanted to brush away the wetness but she wouldn't let my hands go. "You see what I'm telling you? You're young . . . don't brush up against me too close. You'll get dirty and you'll get hurt."

She tried to hide the sob in her throat but couldn't. It came up anyway and I made her let my hands go and when she did I wrapped them around her and held her tight against me. "Helen," I said. "Helen . . ."

She looked at me, grinned weakly. "We must make a funny pair," she said. "Run for it, Joe. Don't stay around any longer."

When I didn't answer right away her eyes looked at mine. I could see her starting to frown a little bit and the curious bewilderment crept across her face. Her mouth was red and moist, poised as if she were going to ask a question, but had forgotten what it was she wanted to say. I let her look and look and look and when she shook her head in a minute gesture of puzzlement I said, "Helen . . . I've rubbed against you. No dirt came off. Maybe it's because I'm no better than you think you are."

"Joe . . ."

"It never happened to me before, kid. When it happens I sure pick a good one for it to happen with." I ran my fingers through her hair. It was nice looking at her like that. Not down, not up, but right into her eyes. "I don't have any family to introduce you to, but if I had, I would. Yellow head, don't worry about me getting hurt."

Her eyes were wide now as if she had the answer. She wasn't believing what she saw.

"I love you, Helen. It's not the way a boy would love anybody. It's a peculiar kind of thing I never want to change."

Joe . . ."

"But it's yours now. You have to decide. Look at me, kid. Then say it."

Those lovely wide eyes grew misty again and the smile came back slowly. It was a warm, radiant smile that told me more than her words. "It can happen to us, can't it? Perhaps it's happened before to somebody else, but it can happen to *us*, can't it? Joe . . . It seems so . . . I can't describe it. There's something . . ."

"Say it out."

"I love you, Joe. Maybe it's better that I should love a little boy. Twenty . . . twenty-one you said? Oh, please, please don't let it be wrong, please . . ." She pressed herself to me with a deep-throated sob and clung there. My fingers rubbed her neck, ran across the width of her shoulders then I pushed her away. I was grinning a little bit now.

"In eighty years it won't make much difference," I said. Then what else I had to say her mouth cut off like a burning torch that tried to seek out the answer and when it was over it didn't seem important enough to mention anyway.

I pushed her away gently. "Now, listen, there isn't much time. I want you to stay here. Don't go out at all and if you want anything, have it sent up. When I come back, I'll knock once. Just once. Keep that door locked and stay out of sight. You got that?"

"Yes, but . . ."

"Don't worry about me. I won't be long. Just remember to make sure it's me and nobody else." I grinned at her. "You aren't getting away from me any more, blondie. Now it's the two of us for keeps, together."

"All right, Joe."

I nudged her chin with my fist, held her face up and kissed it. That curious look was back and she was trying to think of something again. I grinned, winked at her and got out before she could keep me. I even grinned at the clerk downstairs, but he didn't grin back. He probably thought anybody who'd leave a blonde like that alone was nuts or married and he wasn't used to it.

But it sure felt good. You know how. You feel so good you want to tear something apart or laugh and maybe a little crazy, but that's all part of it. That's how I was feeling until I remembered the other things and knew what I had to do.

I found a gin mill down the street and changed a buck into a handful of coins. Three of them got my party and I said, "Mr. Carboy?"

"That's right. Who is this?"

"Joe Boyle."

Carboy told somebody to be quiet then, "What do you want, kid?"

I got the pitch as soon as I caught the tone in his voice. "Your boys haven't got me, if that's what you're thinking," I told him.

"Yeah?"

"I didn't take a powder. I was trying to get something done. For once figure somebody else got brains too."

"You weren't supposed to do any thinking, kid."

"Well, if I don't, you lose a boatload of merchandise, friend."

"What?" It was a whisper that barely came

through.

"Renzo's ticking you off. He and Gulley are pulling a switch. Your stuff gets delivered to him."

"Knock it off, kid. What do you know?"

"I know the boat's coming into the slipside docks with the load and Renzo will be picking it up. You hold the bag, brother."

"Joe," he said. "You know what happens if you're queering me."

"I know."

"Where'd you pick it up?"

"Let's say I sat in on Renzo's conference with Gulley."

"Okay, boy. I'll stick with it. You better be right. Hold on." He turned away from the phone and shouted muffled orders at someone. There were more muffled shouts in the background then he got back on the line again. "Just one thing more. What about Vetter?"

"Not yet, Mr. Carboy. Not yet."

"You get some of my boys to stick with you. I don't like my plans interfered with. Where are you?"

"In a place called Patty's. A gin mill."

"I know it. Stay there ten minutes. I'll shoot a couple guys down. You got that handkerchief yet?"

"Still in my pocket."

"Good. Keep your eyes open."

He slapped the phone back and left me there. I checked the clock on the wall, went to the bar and had an orange, then when the ten minutes were up, drifted outside. I was half a block away when a car door slapped shut and I heard the steady tread of footsteps across the street.

Now it was set. Now the big blow. The show ought to be good when it happened and I wanted to see it happen. There was a cab stand at the end of the block and I hopped in the one on the end. He nodded when I gave him the address, looked at the bill in my hand and took off. In back of us the lights of another car prowled through the night, but always looking our way.

You smelt the place before you reached it. On one side the darkened store fronts were like sleeping drunks, little ones and big ones in a jumbled mass, but all smelling the same. There was the fish smell and on top that of wood the salt spray had started to rot. The bay stretched out endlessly on the other side, a few boats here and there marked with running lights, the rest just vague silhouettes against the sky. In the distance the moon turned the train trestle into a giant spidery hand. The white sign, SLIPSIDE, pointed on the dock area and I told the driver to turn up the street and keep right on going. I picked the bill from my fingers, slowed around the turn, then picked it up when I hopped out. In a few seconds the other car came by, made the turn and lost itself further up the street. When it was gone I stepped out of the shadows and crossed over. Maybe thirty seconds later the car came tearing back up the street again and I ducked back into a doorway. Phil Carboy was going to be pretty sore at those boys of his.

I stood still when I reached the corner again and listened. It was too quiet. You could hear the things that scurried around on the dock. The things were even bold enough to cross the street and one was dragging something in its mouth. Another, a curious elongated creature whose fur shone silvery in the street light pounced on it and the two fought and squealed until the raider had what it went after.

It happens even with rats, I thought. Who learns from who? Do the rats watch the men or the men watch the rats?

Another one of them ran into the gutter. It was going to cross, then stood on its hind legs in an attitude of attention, its face pointing toward the dock. I never saw it move, but it disappeared, then I heard what it had heard, carefully muffled sounds, then a curse not so muffled.

It came too quick to say it had a starting

point. First the quick stab of orange and the sharp thunder of the gun, then the others following and the screams of the slugs whining off across the water. They didn't try to be quiet now. There was a startled shout, a hoarse scream and the yell of somebody who was hit.

Somebody put out the street light and the darkness was a blanket that slid in. I could hear them running across the street, then the moon reached down before sliding behind a cloud again and I saw them, a dozen or so closing in on the dock from both sides.

Out on the water an engine barked into life, was gunned and a boat wheeled away down the channel. The car that had been cruising around suddenly dimmed its lights, turned off the street and stopped. I was right there with no place to duck into and feet started running my way. I couldn't go back and there was trouble ahead. The only other thing was to make a break for it across the street and hope nobody spotted me.

I'd pushed it too far. I was being a dope again. One of them yelled and started behind me at a long angle. I. didn't stop at the rail. I went over the side into the water, kicked away from the concrete abutment and hoped I'd come up under the pier. I almost made it. I was a foot away from the piling but it wasn't enough. When I looked back the guy was there at the rail with a gun bucking in his hand and the bullets were walking up the water toward me. He must have still had a half load left and only a foot to go when another shot blasted out over my head and the guy grabbed at his face with a scream and fell back to the street. The guy up above said, "Get the son . . ." and the last word had a whistle to it as something caught him in the belly. He was all doubled up when he hit the water and his tombstone was a tiny trail of bubbles that broke the surface a few seconds before stopping altogether.

I pulled myself further under the dock. From where I was I could hear the voices and now they had quieted down. Out on the street somebody yelled to stand back and before the words were out cut loose with a sharp blast of an automatic rifle. It gave the bunch on the street time to close in and those on the dock scurried back further.

Right over my head the planks were warped away and when a voice said, "I found it," I could pick Johnny's voice out of the racket.

"Where?"

"Back ten feet on the pole. Better hop to it before they get wise and cut the wires."

Johnny moved fast and I tried to move with him. By the time I reached the next piling I could hear him dialing the phone. He talked fast, but kept his voice down. *"Renzo? Yeah, they bottled us. Somebody pulled the cork out of the deal. Yeah. The hell with that, you call the cops. Let them break it up.* Sure, sure. Move it. We can make it to one of the boats. They got Tommy and Balco. Two of the others were hit but not bad. Yeah, it's Carboy all right. He ain't here himself, but they're his guys. Yeah, I got the stuff. Shake it."

His feet pounded on the planking overhead and I could hear his voice without making out what he said. The next minute the blasting picked up and I knew they were trying for a stand off. Whatever they had for cover up there must have been pretty good because the guys on the street were swearing at it and yelling for somebody to spread out and get them from the sides. The only trouble was that there was no protection on the street and if the moon came out again they'd be nice easy targets.

It was the moan of the siren that stopped it. First one, then another joined in and I heard them running for the cars. A man screamed and yelled for them to take it easy. Something rattled over my head and when I looked up, a frame of black marred the flooring. Something was rolled to the edge, then crammed over. Another followed it. Men. Dead. They bobbed for a minute, then sank slowly. Somebody said, "Damn, I hate to do that. He was okay."

"Shut up and get out there." It was Johnny.

The voice said, "Yeah, come on, you," then they went over the side. I stayed back of the piling and watched them swim for the boats. The sirens were coming closer now. One had a lead as if it knew the way and the others didn't. Johnny didn't come down. I grinned to myself, reached for a cross-brace and swung up on it. From there it was easy to make the trapdoor.

And there was Johnny by the end of the pier squatting down behind a packing case that seemed to be built around some machinery, squatting with that tenseness of a guy about to run. He had a box in his arms about two feet square and when I said, "Hello, chum," he stood up so fast he dropped it, but he would have had to do that anyway the way he was reaching for his rod.

He almost had it when I belted him across the nose. I got him with another sharp hook and heard the breath hiss out of him. It spun him around until the packing case caught him and when I was coming in he let me have it with his foot. I skidded sidewise, took the toe of his shoe on my hip then had his arm in a lock that brought a scream tearing out of his throat. He was going for the rod again when the arm broke and in a crazy surge of pain he jerked loose, tripped me, and got the gun out with his good hand. I rolled into his feet as it coughed over my head, grabbed his wrist and turned it into his neck and he pulled the trigger for the last time in trying to get his hand loose. There was just one last, brief, horrified expression in his eyes as he looked at me, then they filmed over to start rotting away.

The siren that was screaming turned the corner with its wail dying out. Brakes squealed against the pavement and the car stopped, the red light on its hood snapping shut. The door opened opposite the driver, stayed open as if the one inside was listening. Then a guy crawled out, a little guy with a big gun in his hand. He said, "Johnny?"

Then he ran. Silently, like an Indian, I almost had Johnny's gun back in my hand when he reached me.

"You," Sergeant Gonzales said. He saw the package there, twisted his mouth into a smile and let me see the hole in the end of his gun. I still made one last try for Johnny's gun when the blast went off. I half expected the sickening smash of a bullet, but none came. When I looked up, Gonzales was still there. Something on the packing crate had hooked into his coat and held him up.

I couldn't see into the shadows where the voice came from. But it was a familiar voice. It said, "You ought to be careful son."

The gun the voice held slithered back into leather.

"Thirty seconds. No more. You might even do the job right and beat it in his car. He was in on it. The cop . . . he was working with Cooley. Then Cooley ran out on him too so he played along with Renzo. Better move, kid."

The other sirens were almost there. I said, "Watch yourself. And thanks."

"Sure, kid. I hate crooked cops worse than crooks."

I ran for the car, hopped in and pulled the door shut. Behind me something splashed and a two foot square package floated on the water a moment, then turned over and sunk out of sight. I left the lights off, turned down the first street I reached and headed across town. At the main drag I pulled up, wiped the wheel and gearshift free of prints and got out.

There was dawn showing in the sky. It would be another hour yet before it was morning. I. walked until I reached the junkyard in back of Gordon's office, found the wreck of a car that still had cushions in it, climbed in and went to sleep.

Morning, afternoon, then evening. I slept

through the first two. The last one was harder. I sat there thinking things, keeping out of sight. My clothes were dry now, but the cigarettes still had a lousy taste. There was a twinge in my stomach and my mouth was dry. I gave it another hour before I moved, then went back over the fence and down the street to a dirty little diner that everybody avoided except the boys who rode the rods into town. I knocked off a plate of bacon and eggs, paid for it with some of the change I had left, picked up a pack of butts and started out. That was when I saw the paper on the table.

It made quite a story. GANG WAR FLARES ON WATERFRONT, and under it a subhead that said, *Cop, Hoodlum, Slain in Gun Duel.* It was a masterpiece of writing that said nothing, intimated much and brought out the fact that though the place was bullet-sprayed and though evidence of other wounded was found, there were no bodies to account for what had happened. One sentence mentioned the fact that Johnny was connected with Mark Renzo. The press hinted at police inefficiency. There was the usual statement from Captain Gerot.

The thing stunk. Even the press was afraid to talk out. How long would it take to find out Gonzales didn't die by a shot from Johnny's gun? Not very long. And Johnny . . . a cute little twist like that would usually get a big splash. There wasn't even any curiosity shown about Johnny. I let out a short laugh and threw the paper back again.

They were like rats, all right. They just went the rats one better. They dragged their bodies away with them so there wouldn't be any ties. Nice. Now find the doctor who patched them up. Find what they were after on the docks. Maybe they figured to heist ten tons or so of machinery. Yeah, try and find it.

No, they wouldn't say anything. Maybe they'd have to hit it a little harder when the big one broke. When the boys came in who paid a few million out for a package that was never delivered. Maybe when the big trouble came and the blood ran again somebody would crawl back out of his hole long enough to put it into print. Or it could be that Bucky Edwards was right. Life was too precious a thing to sell cheaply.

I thought about it, remembering everything he had told me. When I had it all back in my head again I turned toward the place where I knew Bucky would be and walked faster. Halfway there it started to drizzle. I turned up the collar of my coat.

It was a soft rain, one of those things that comes down at the end of summer, making its own music like a dull concert you think will have no end. It drove people indoors until even the cabs didn't bother to cruise. The cars that went by had their windows steamed into opaque squares, the drivers peering through the hand-wiped panes.

I jumped a streetcar when one came along, took it downtown and got off again. And I was back with the people I knew and the places made for them. Bucky was on his usual stool and I wondered if it was a little too late. He had that all gone look in his face and his fingers were caressing a tall amber-colored glass.

When I sat down next to him his eyes moved, giving me a glassy stare. It was like the cars on the street, they were cloudy with mist, then a hand seemed to reach out and rub them clear. They weren't glass any more. I could see the white in his fingers as they tightened around the glass and he said, "You did it fancy, kiddo. Get out of here."

"Scared, Bucky?"

His eyes went past me to the door, then came back again. "Yes. You said it right. I'm scared. Get out. I don't want to be around when they find you."

"For a guy who's crocked most of the time you seem to know a lot about what happens."

"I think a lot. I figure it out. There's only one answer."

"If you know it why don't you write it?"

"Living's not much fun any more, but what there is of it, I like. Beat it, kid."

This time I grinned at him, a big fat grin and told the bartender to get me an orange. Large. He shoved it down, picked up my dime and went back to his paper.

I said, "Let's hear about it, Bucky." I could feel my mouth changing the grin into something else. "I don't like to be a target either. I want to know the score."

Bucky's tongue made a pass over dry lips. He seemed to look back inside himself to something he had been a long time ago, dredging the memory up. He found himself in the mirror behind the back bar, twisted his mouth at it and looked back at me again.

"This used to be a good town."

"Not that," I said.

He didn't hear me. "Now anybody who knows anything is scared to death. To death, I said. Let them talk and that's what they get. Death. From one side or another. It was bad enough when Renzo took over, worse when Carboy came in. It's not over yet." His shoulders made an involuntary shudder and he pulled the drink halfway down the glass. "Friend Gulley had an accident this afternoon. He was leaving town and was run off the road. He's dead."

I whistled softly. "Who?"

For the first time a trace of humor put lines at the corner of his lips. "It wasn't Renzo. It wasn't Phil Carboy. They were all accounted for. The tire marks are very interesting. It looked like the guy wanted to stop friend Gulley for a chat but Gulley hit the ditch. You could call it a real accident without lying." He finished the rest of the drink, put it down and said, "The boys are scared stiff." He looked at me closely then. "Vetter," he said.

"He's getting close."

Bucky didn't hear me. "I'm getting to like the guy. He does what should have been done a long time ago. By himself he does it. They know who killed Gonzales. One of Phil's boys saw it happen before he ran for it. There's a guy with a broken neck who was found out on the highway and they know who did that and how." He swirled the ice around in his glass. "He's taking good care of you, kiddo."

I didn't say anything.

"There's just one little catch to it, Joe. One little catch."

"What?"

"That boy who saw Gonzales get it saw something else. He saw you and Johnny tangle over the package. He figures you got it. Everybody knows and now they want you. It can't happen twice. Renzo wants it and Carboy wants it. You know who gets it?"

I shook my head.

"You get it. In the belly or in the head. Even the cops want you that bad. Captain Gerot even thinks that way. You better get out of here, Joe. Keep away from me. There's something about you that spooks me. Something in the way your eyes look. Something about your face. I wish I could see into that mind of yours. I always thought I knew people, but I don't know you at all. You spook me. You should see your own eyes. I've seen eyes like yours before but I can't remember where. They're familiar as hell, but I can't place them. They don't belong in a kid's face at all. Go on, Joe, beat it. The boys are all over town. They got orders to do just one thing. Find you. When they do I don't want you sitting next to me."

"When do you write the big story, Bucky?"

"You tell me."

My teeth were tight together with the smile moving around them. "It won't be long."

"No . . . maybe just a short obit. They're tracking you fast. That hotel was no cover at all. Do it smarter the next time."

The ice seemed to pour down all over me. It went down over my shoulders, ate through my skin until it was in the blood that pounded through my body. I grabbed his arm and damn near jerked him off the stool. "What about the hotel?"

All he did was shrug. Bucky was gone again.

I cursed silently, ran back into the rain again and down the block to the cab stand.

The clerk said he was sorry, he didn't know anything about room 612. The night man had taken a week off. I grabbed the key from his hand and pounded up the stairs. All I could feel was that mad frenzy of hate swelling in me and I kept saying her name over and over to myself. I threw the door open, stood there breathing fast while I called myself a dozen different kinds of fool.

She wasn't there. It was empty.

A note lay beside the telephone. All it said was, *"Bring it where you brought the first one."*

I laid the note down again and stared out the window into the night. There was sweat on the backs of my hands. Bucky had called it. They thought I had the package and they were forcing a trade. Then Mark Renzo would kill us both. He thought.

I brought the laugh up from way down in my throat. It didn't sound much like me at all. I looked at my hands and watched them open and close into fists. There were callouses across the palms, huge things that came from

Gordon's junk carts. A year and a half of it, I thought. Eighteen months of pushing loads of scrap iron for pennies then all of a sudden I was part of a multi-million dollar operation. The critical part of it. I was the enigma. Me, Joey the junk pusher. Not even Vetter now. Just me. Vetter would come when they had me out of the way.

For a while I stared at the street. That tiny piece of luck that chased me caught up again and I saw the car stop and the men jump out. One was Phil Carboy's right hand man. In a way it was funny. Renzo was always a step ahead of the challenger, but Phil was coming up fast. He'd caught on too and was ready to pull the same deal. He didn't know it had already been pulled.

But that was all right too.

I reached for the pen on the desk, lifted a sheet of cheap stationary out of the drawer and scrawled across it, *"Joe . . . be back in a few hours. Stay here with the package until I return. I'll have the car ready."* I signed it, *Helen*, put it by the phone and picked up the receiver.

The clerk said, "Yes?"

I said, "In a minute some men will come in looking for the blonde and me. You think the room is empty, but let them come up. You haven't seen me at all yet. Understand?"

"Say ..."

"Mister, if you want to walk out of here tonight you'll do what you're told. You're liable to get killed otherwise. Understand that?"

I hung up and let him think about it. I'd seen his type before and I wasn't worried a bit. I got out, locked the door and started up the stairs to the roof. It didn't take me longer than five minutes to reach the street and when I turned the corner the light was back on in the room I had just left. I gave it another five minutes and the tall guy came out again, spoke to the driver of the car and the fellow reached in and shut off the engine. It had worked. The light in the window went out. The vigil had started and the boys could afford to be pretty patient. They thought.

The rain was a steady thing coming down just a little bit harder than it had. It was cool and fresh with the slightest nip in it. I walked, putting the pieces together in my head. I did it slowly, replacing the fury that had been there, deliberately wiping out the gnawing worry that tried to grow. I reached the deserted square of the park and picked out a bench under a tree and sat there letting the rain drip down around me. When I looked at my hands they were shaking.

I was thinking wrong. I should have been

thinking about fat, ugly faces; rat faces with deep voices and whining faces. I should have been thinking about the splashes of orange a rod makes when it cuts a man down and blood on the street. Cops who want the big pay off. Thinking of a town where even the press was cut of and the big boys came from the city to pick up the stuff that started more people on the long slide down to the grave.

Those were the things I should have thought of.

All I could think of was Helen. Lovely Helen who had been all things to many men and hated it. Beautiful Helen who didn't want me to be hurt, who was afraid the dirt would rub off. Helen who found love for the first time . . . and me. The beauty in her face when I told her. Beauty that waited to be kicked and wasn't because I loved her too much and didn't give a damn what she had been. She was different now. Maybe I was too. She didn't know it, but she was the good one, not me. She was the child that needed taking care of, not me. Now she was hours away from being dead and so was I. The thing they wanted, the thing that could buy her life I saw floating in the water beside the dock. It was like having a yacht with no fuel aboard.

The police? No, not them. They'd want me. They'd think it was a phoney. That wasn't the answer. Not Phil Carboy either. He was after the same thing Renzo was.

I started to laugh, it was so damn, pathetically funny. I had it all in my hand and couldn't turn it around. What the devil does a guy have to do? How many times does he have to kill himself? The answer. It was right there but wouldn't come through. It wasn't the same answer I had started with, but a better one.

So I said it all out to myself. Out loud, with words. I started with the night I brought the note to Renzo, the one that promised him Vetter would cut his guts out. I even described their faces to myself when Vetter's name was mentioned. One name, that's all it took, and you could see the fear creep in because Vetter was deadly and unknown. He was the shadow that stood there, the one they couldn't trust, the one they all knew in the society that stayed outside the law. He was a high-priced killer who never missed and always got more than he was paid to take. So deadly they'd give anything to keep him out of town, even to doing the job he was there for. So deadly they could throw me or anybody else to the wolves just to finger him. So damn deadly they put an army on him, yet so deadly he could move behind their lines without any trouble at all.

Vetter.

I cursed the name. I said Helen's. Vetter wasn't important any more. Not to me.

The rain lashed at my face as I looked up into it. The things I knew fell into place and I knew what the answer was. I remembered something I didn't know was there, a sign on the docks by the fishing fleet that said "SEASON LOCKERS."

Jack Cooley had been smart by playing it simple. He even left me the ransom.

I got up, walked to the corner and waited until a cab came by. I flagged him down, got in and gave the address of the white house where Cooley had lived.

The same guy answered the door. He took the bill from my hand and nodded me in. I said, "Did he leave any old clothes behind at all?"

"Some fishing stuff downstairs. It's behind the coal bin. You want that?"

"I want that," I said.

He got up and I followed him. He switched on the cellar light, took me downstairs and across the littered pile of refuse a cellar can collect. When he pointed to the old set of dungarees on the nail in the wall, I went over and felt through the pockets. The key was in the jacket. I said thanks and went back upstairs. The taxi was still waiting. He flipped his butt away when I got in, threw the heap into gear and headed toward the smell of the water.

I had to climb the fence to get on the pier.

There wasn't much to it. The lockers were tall steel affairs, each with somebody's name scrawled across it in chalk. The number that matched the key didn't say Cooley, but it didn't matter any more either. I opened it up and saw the cardboard box that had been jammed in there so hard it had snapped one of the rods in the corner. Just to be sure I pulled one end open, tore through the other box inside and tasted the white powder it held.

Heroin.

They never expected Cooley to do it so simply. He had found a way to grab their load and stashed it without any trouble at all. Friend Jack was good at that sort of thing. Real clever. Walked away with a couple million bucks' worth of stuff and never lived to convert it. He wasn't quite smart enough. Not quite as smart as Carboy, Gerot, Renzo . . . or even a kid who pushed a junk cart. Smart enough to grab the load, but not smart enough to keep on living.

I closed the locker and went back over the fence with the box in my arms. The cabbie found me a phone in a gin mill and waited while I made my calls. The first one got me Gerot's home number. The second got me Captain Gerot himself, a very annoyed Gerot who had been pulled out of bed.

I said, "Captain, this is Joe Boyle and if you

trace this call you're going to scramble the whole deal."

So the captain played it smart. "Go ahead," was all he told me.

"You can have them all. Every one on a platter. You know what I'm talking about?"

"I know."

"You want it that way?"

"I want you, Joe. Just you."

"I'll give you that chance. First you have to take the rest. There won't be any doubt this time. They won't be big enough to crawl out of it. There isn't enough money to buy them out either. You'll have every one of them cold."

"I'll still want you."

I laughed at him. "I said you'll get your chance. All you have to do is play it my way. You don't mind that, do you?"

"Not if I get you, Joe."

I laughed again. "You'll need a dozen men. Ones you can trust. Ones who can shoot straight and aren't afraid of what might come later."

"I can get them."

"Have them stand by. It won't be long. I'll call again."

I hung up, stared at the phone a second, then went back outside. The cabbie was working his way through another cigarette. I said, "I need a fast car. Where do I get one?"

"How fast for how much?"

"The limit."

"I got a friend with a souped-up Ford. Nothing can touch it. It'll cost you."

I showed him the thing in my hand. His eyes narrowed at the edges. "Maybe it won't cost you at that," he said. He looked at me the same way Helen had, then waved me in.

We made a stop at an out of the way rooming house. I kicked my clothes off and climbed into some fresh stuff, then tossed everything else into a bag and woke up the landlady of the place. I told her to mail it to the post office address on the label and gave her a few bucks for her trouble. She promised me she would, took the bag into her room and I went outside. I felt better in the suit. I patted it down to make sure everything was set. The cabbie shot me a half smile when he saw me and held the door open.

I got the Ford and it didn't cost me a thing unless I piled it up. The guy grinned when he handed me the keys and made a familiar gesture with his hand. I grinned back. I gave the cabbie his fare with a little extra and got in the Ford with my box. It was almost over.

A mile outside Mark Renzo's roadhouse I stopped at a gas station and while the attendant filled me up all around, I used his phone. I got

Renzo on the first try and said, "This is Joe, fat boy."

His breath in the phone came louder than the words. "Where are you?"

"Never mind. I'll be there. Let me talk to Helen."

I heard him call and then there was Helen. Her voice was tired and all the hope was gone from it. She said, "Joe . . ."

It was enough. I'd know her voice any time. I said, "Honey . . . don't worry about it. You'll be okay."

She started to say something else, but Renzo must have grabbed the phone from her. "You got the stuff, kid?"

"I got it."

"Let's go, sonny. You know what happens if you don't."

"I know," I said. "You better do something first. I want to see the place of yours empty in a hurry. I don't feel like being stopped going in. Tell them to drive out and keep on going. I'll deliver the stuff to you, that's all."

"Sure, kid, sure. You'll see the boys leave."

"I'll be watching," I said.

Joke.

I made the other call then. It went back to my hotel room and I did it smart. I heard the phone ring when the clerk hit the room number, heard the phone get picked up and said as though I were in one big hurry, *"Look, Helen, I'm hopping the stuff out to Renzo's. He's waiting for it. As soon as he pays off we'll blow. See you later."*

When I slapped the phone back I laughed again then got Gerot again. This time he was waiting. I said, "Captain . . . they'll all be at Renzo's place. There'll be plenty of fun for everybody. You'll even find a fortune in heroin."

"You're the one I want, Joe."

"Not even Vetter?"

"No, he comes next. First you." This time he hung up on me. So I laughed again as the joke got funnier and made my last call.

The next voice was the one I had come to know so well. I said, "Joe Boyle. I'm heading for Renzo's. Cooley had cached the stuff in a locker and I need it for a trade. I have a light blue Ford and need a quick way out. The trouble is going to start."

"There's a side entrance," the voice said. They don't use it any more. If you're careful you can come in that way and if you stay careful you can make it to the big town without getting spotted."

"I heard about Gulley," I said.

"Saddening. He was a wealthy man."

"You'll be here?"

"Give me five minutes," the voice told me. "I'll be at the side entrance. I'll make sure nobody stops you."

"There'll be police. They won't be asking questions."

"Let me take care of that."

"Everybody wants Vetter," I said.

"Naturally. Do you think they'll find him?"

I grinned. "I doubt it."

The other voice chuckled as it hung up.

I saw them come out from where I stood in the bushes. They got into cars, eight of them and drove down the drive slowly. They turned back toward town and I waited until their lights were a mile away before I went up the steps of the club.

At that hour it was an eerie place, a dimly lit ghost house showing the signs of people that had been there earlier. I stood inside the door, stopped and listened. Up the stairs I heard a cough. It was like that first night, only this time I didn't have somebody dragging me. I could remember the stairs and the long, narrow corridor at the top, and the oak panelled door at the end of it. Even the thin line of light that came from under the door. I snuggled the box under my arm and walked in.

Renzo was smiling from his chair behind the

desk. It was a funny kind of a smile like I was a sucker. Helen was huddled on the floor in a corner holding a hand to the side of her cheek. Her dress had been shredded down to the waist, and tendrils of tattered cloth clung to the high swell of her breasts, followed the smooth flow of her body. Her other hand tried desperately to hide her nakedness from Renzo's leer. She was trembling, and the terror in her eyes was an ungodly thing.

And Renzo grinned. Big, fat Renzo. Renzo the louse whose eyes were now on the package under my arm, with the grin turning to a slow sneer. Renzo the killer who found a lot of ways to get away with murder and was looking at me as if he were seeing me for the first time.

He said, "You got your going away clothes on, kid."

"Yeah."

"You won't be needing them." He made the sneer bigger, but I wasn't watching him. I was watching Helen, seeing the incredible thing that crossed her face.

"I'm different, Helen?"

She couldn't speak. All she could do was nod.

"I told you I wasn't such a kid. I just look that way. Twenty . . . twenty-one you thought?" I laughed and it had a funny sound. Renzo stopped sneering. "I got ten years on that, honey. Don't worry about being in love with a kid."

Renzo started to get up then. Slowly, a ponderous monster with hands spread apart to kill something. "You two did it. You damn near ruined me. You know what happens now?" He licked his lips and the muscles rolled under his shirt.

My face was changing shape and I nodded. Renzo never noticed. Helen saw it. I said, "A lot happens now, fat boy." I dropped the package on the floor and kicked it to one side. Renzo moved out from behind the desk. He wasn't thinking any more. He was just seeing me and thinking of his empire that had almost toppled. The package could set it up again. I said, "Listen, you can hear it happen."

Then he stopped to think. He turned his head and you could hear the whine of engines and the shots coming clear across the night through the rain. There was a frenzy about the way it was happening, the frenzy and madness that goes into a banzai charge and above it the moan of sirens that seemed to go ignored.

It was happening to Renzo too, the kill hate in his eyes, the saliva that made wet paths from the corners of his tight mouth. His whole body heaved and when his head turned back to me again, the eyes were bright with the lust of murder.

I said, "Come here, Helen," and she came to me. I took the envelope out of my pocket and gave it to her, and then I took off my jacket, slipping it over her shoulders. She pulled it closed over her breasts, the terror in her eyes fading. "Go out the side . . . the old road. The car is waiting there. You'll see a tall guy beside it, a big guy all around and if you happen to see his face, forget it. Tell him this. Tell him I said to give the report to the Chief. Tell him to wait until I contact him for the next assignment then start the car and wait for me. I'll be in a hurry. You got that?"

"Yes, Joe." The disbelief was still in her eyes.

Renzo moved slowly, the purpose plain in his face. His hands were out and he circled between me and the door. There was something fiendish about his face.

The sirens and the shooting were getting closer.

He said, "Vetter won't get you out of this, kid. I'm going to kill you and it'll be the best thing I ever did. Then the dame. The blonde. Weber told me he saw a blonde at Gulley's and I knew who did this to me. The both of you are going to die, kid. There ain't no Vetter here now."

I let him have a long look at me. I grinned. I said, "Remember what that note said? It said

Vetter was going to spill your guts all over the floor. You remember that, Renzo?"

"Yeah," He said. "Now tell me you got a gun, kid. Tell me that and I'll tell you you're a liar. I can smell a rod a mile away. You had it, kid. There ain't no Vetter here now."

Maybe it was the way I let myself go. I could feel the loosening in my shoulders and my face was a picture only Renzo could see. "You killed too many men, Renzo, one too many. The ones you peddle the dope to die slowly, the ones who take it away die quick. It's still a lot of men. You killed them, Renzo, a whole lot of them. You know what happens to killers in this country? It's a funny law, but it works. Sometimes to get what it wants, it works in peculiar fashion. But it works.

"Remember the note. Remember hard what it said." I grinned and what was in it stopped him five feet away. What was in it made him frown, then his eyes opened wide, almost too wide and he had the expression Helen had the first time.

I said to her, "Don't wait, Helen," and heard the door open and close. Renzo was backing away, his feet shuffling on the carpet.

Two minutes at the most.

"I'm Vetter," I said. "Didn't you know? Couldn't you tell? Me . . . Vetter. The one everybody wonders about, even the cops. Vetter the puzzle. Vetter the one who's there but isn't there." The air was cold against my teeth. "Remember the note, Renzo. No, you can't smell a gun because I haven't got one. But look at my hand. You're big and strong . . . you're a killer, but look at my hand and find out who the specialist really is and you'll know that there was no lie in that note you read the first night."

Renzo tried to scream, stumbled and fell. I laughed again and moved in on him. He was reaching for something in the desk drawer knowing all the time that he wasn't going to make it and the knife in my hand made a nasty little snick and he screamed again so high it almost blended with the sirens.

Maybe one minute left, but it would be enough and the puzzle would always be there and the name when mentioned would start another ball rolling and the country a little cleaner and the report when the Chief read it would mean one more done with . . . done differently, but done.

TO THE READER

If you enjoyed this book, you will be glad to know that there are many others just as well written, just as interesting, to be had in the Fiction House Press Library.

You will find the Fiction House Press Library online at

www.FictionHousePress.com

Made in the USA
Las Vegas, NV
20 September 2022